In Her Shadow

In Her Shadow
Marianne Murray

To Stacey
I hope you enjoy
the story!
love,
Marianne
xxx

In Her Shadow

Born and raised in Scotland, Marianne started out; wanting to be a dancer.

Her dreams changed when she discovered acting and so, she then wanted to be an actress.

Writing this book at age 25, she dreamed a new dream; she wants to be a writer also. She wants to have her cake and eat it too and, why the hell not?

Acknowledgements

This story came to me in a dream and although it is a work of fiction; there are people in my life who have inspired certain traits of the characters.

I always try to write what I know and in doing this; sometimes, the lines between fact and fiction blur.

I believe I have remained as true to my dream as possible. It was a very sad dream but it was lovely to get it down on paper and I have to thank those who; have encouraged, inspired and believed in me, along the way.

Your support means the world. Without it, I'd still be staring at a blank page and wondering, 'Can I actually do this?'

Thank you for answering, 'Yes, you can'.

In Her Shadow

For, my mum and dad.
Even in my hours of procrastination,
they believed in me still.
I love you both. Millions.
Thank you.
~

Prologue

It's a wet and windy afternoon in October – four days from Halloween – and Danny has just finished his job as a history teacher for the day.

He pulls his collar up, trying to garner as much heat as possible but failing, as the wind is much too strong and it chills him to the bone.

He contemplates going somewhere for a nice, steaming cup of coffee to warm him but before he can decide where to go, his gaze is pulled to a little window across the street from him. He looks at the sign above the window which reads, "Jenny's Dream" and he chuckles to himself.

Finding it amusing that a place as small and as desolate as this, could be anyone's idea of a dream. He is about to move on to what he would consider a better place to drink his coffee but before he takes a step forward; his eyes are drawn back once more, to the window. This time, to what lies beyond it.

A girl, not astoundingly beautiful – not his usual type – but alluring all the same, captures his attention as she smiles out to him. A smile that somehow gives him the warmth he was searching for and before he knows what he is doing, he is making his way inside and taking a seat, close to the counter.

In Her Shadow

Chapter 1: Milk, No Sugar

"Hello, I'm jenny and I will be your server for today."
The girl says, smiling.
"Would you like a menu or do you know what you are having?"
Danny looks up at her in awe, as if he has just met the most famous person on the planet and all he can do is nod his head and smile back. She takes this as indication that he would like a menu and so hands one to him.
She gifts him another warm smile before she turns and takes the order of someone who knows what they want. Danny decides he would only like a coffee and waits patiently for her to return.
While waiting, he lets his eyes soak up every part of her. From her big, green eyes, to the way she blows her fringe out of her face; she gives him butterflies.
"Do you know what you want yet, sir?"
She asks, notepad at the ready.
"Danny."
He replies.
"Sorry?"
"My name, it's Danny."
She nods her head and smiles.
"Oh, right!"
She says, and taps her pen gently against her lips.
"Do you know what you would like, Danny?"
The butterflies is his tummy multiply as he likes the way she said his name.
"Just a coffee. Milk, no sugar."

He responds, his words rushed.

"Because you're sweet enough?"

He blushes at this and nods his head.

"I figured so."

    She says, playing friendly.

"One milky coffee coming right up."

She dashes away to make his order and when she returns; he tries to think of something to say, to spark up some conversation.

"So, this is your dream?"

He asks, looking around.

"You're the Jenny on the sign?"

Now Jenny blushes.

"It's silly, isn't it?"

She sighs.

"It was always my dream to run my own diner, like the ones you see in the movies and when the day came for me to make that dream a reality, I was short on creativity."

He smiles.

"No, that's not silly at all."

He says, shaking his head.

"How long have you been here?"

Jenny tries to add it up on her fingers, mouthing the months as she does so.

"It'll be two years in January, I think."

She says.

"Sometimes I'm so rushed off of my feet that, all the days just merge into one."

Danny nods.

"That's... good."

He says, looking around awkwardly as he is out of conversation.

"I think you have a customer."

In Her Shadow

Jenny turns to see an old man waiting at the counter.

"I better get back to work, enjoy your coffee."

She says, perking herself up once more.

"Thank you. It was nice meeting you, Jenny."

She blows her fringe out of her eyes.

"You too."

She replies, and she has already forgotten his name so she feels a bit embarrassed.

"Please, do come again."

She adds, trying to make him feel a little special so that she could gain another customer.

After the old man, it seemed people just started to flood through the door and Jenny didn't get another minute to even look at Danny, never mind chat with him. He thought about leaving his number on the napkin, maybe with a little note saying how he would like to get to know her but he didn't want to come across as that creepy guy at the diner so; he decides against it and anyway, he knows he will be back here again and there would be plenty of time then.

He steps back out into the cold which chills him even more so now, that he's spent some time heating up.

On his way home, he thinks about Jenny and why he felt so drawn to her. Especially when he had never clapped eyes on her before, let alone met her.

He wasn't a believer in love at first sight but what he felt for her was definitely powerful and he thought, maybe it was fate. Maybe he was meant to go there today, meet her and grab hold of his destiny.

Destiny, he believed in. Love at first sight? No way.

But Jenny, she was the type of girl who could make a believer out of such a man.

Chapter 2: Bull In A China Shop

Jenny makes her way down the dairy aisle in her local supermarket; basket in one hand and a little note in the other. She's trying to find a good cheddar to make a nice, comfort meal of macaroni and cheese.

She wanders on, in her own little world and doesn't see the shopping cart in front of her. The person pushing – also in their own little world – doesn't see her.

They collide and Jenny ends up on the floor and before she can be helped up, she springs to her feet, her cheeks red and knees throbbing.

"I'm so sorry!"

She gasps, embarrassed.

"I'm like an elephant shopping in China!"

She exclaims.

"You mean a bull in a China shop."

Jenny feels insulted, thinking the person is being rude about her appearance.

"Okay."

She says sternly.

"You don't have to be so mean. I said I was sorry."

She locks eyes with the man who appears in a stuttering state of mortification and she tries to think where she knows him from.

"No, no! That's the phrase you were looking for."

He mutters.

"I wasn't calling you a bull I-"

She remembers him now.

"Milk, no sugar, right?"

In Her Shadow

The man stops stuttering and realizes the person he has just knocked to the floor is none other than Jenny, from 'Jenny's Dream.' He didn't recognize her as she was wearing baggy clothes and her hair was down.

"Jenny! I didn't see-"

"It's okay, it was my fault."

She says, taking the blame.

"I should have been looking where I was going."

Danny waves his hands in front of him.

"No, I take full responsibility."

He says, stealing the blame from her.

"I have wheels."

He points to the wheels of the shopping cart, causing Jenny to burst into a fit of giggles – something she often finds herself doing, when she is nervous –. Danny joins in and the shoppers who pass them by, look at them as if they have gone completely mad.

Suddenly, Jenny stops giggling and is gasping for air. She can't breathe, her face starts to turn more purple than red and Danny stops laughing too and cries for help.

Her hand rattles and shakes as she reaches into her pocket and retrieves an inhaler. Frantically, she sucks on it for dear life and she is able to breathe normally again.

Panic over, crisis averted. Danny's face remains twisted in fear. He can't believe he almost lost her – if she really was close to death, that is – without getting to know her. He scolds himself for that selfish thought and places a strong hand on her shoulder and squeezes.

"Are you okay?"

He asks, concerned.

"I need a good cheddar."

She brushes off the incident. She doesn't want to draw anymore attention to herself and rushes off down the aisle, grabbing the first cheese she could get her hands on and heads to the checkout. She is embarrassed, more embarrassed than she's ever been in her life, she thinks.

The cashier rings up her groceries and she hurries out of the building, thankful for the air that caresses her face and makes it's way into her lungs. She is unaware that Danny is standing behind her, watching her. He has never seen anyone move with such animality before and he is in a trance, as her body expands and contracts as she gulps up the air.

"Do you need a lift?"

Jenny spins round on her heel, startled at the sudden intrusion to her respiration routine.

"N-N-No, thank you."

She stutters.

"I will be okay."

He takes a step closer.

"It's dark and you're unwell. Maybe-"

"I am fine."

"Yeah but-"

She backs away from him.

"Listen, you don't even know me. I don't know you, you could be a serial killer for all I know."

She raises both her hands in front of her, as if to warn him; not to take any more steps towards her.

"I am fine."

She states, once more.

"I can get home on my own."

Her words sting Danny but they aren't untrue. She doesn't know him but on the other hand, he was only trying to be nice. It seemed anytime he tried to be nice, it always backfired on him and so he wonders; why he even bothers at all. It's not in his nature to be nasty though so, he nods his head and backs away.

In Her Shadow

"I'm sorry."
He sighs.
"You're right."
He smiles at her.
"Safe travels, Jenny."

Jenny feels a sudden pang of guilt. She didn't mean to snap at him but she doesn't like people to make a fuss over her. She is the one who looks after others, not the other way around.

"Tell you what."
She smiles back.
"why don't you come by the diner tomorrow and I'll make you a nice cup of coffee. On the house."
She says, nodding like a bobblehead .
"That way, you can see that I got home safe and also, it'll make me feel better for snapping at you."
She drops her head.
"I didn't mean to, I'm really sorry."

This brings a smile to Danny's face. He accepts the apology – she didn't even have to make, he thinks – and he nods.

"That'll be nice."
He says, accepting her invitation.
"I'll see you tomorrow then?"
"If you still have your eyes!"
She replies.
Danny laughs.
"What?"
She shakes her head.
"I'm not good at jokes. Yes, you'll see me tomorrow."

They both exchange an awkward smile before heading in opposite directions.

Jenny starts to wonder about Danny, whether his intentions are on the good or bad side and if it really was just a coincidence; she met him in her local supermarket, a day after he wandered into her diner. She doesn't let it trouble her for too long. She was trying not to obsess over every little thing these days but still, she had her reservations about the kind stranger.

Danny thinks about what tomorrow will hold, as he drives home. Will he finally get a chance to get to know Jenny, would she even like him if she did know him? His tummy starts to flip and he tries not to think about it but he can't help it, he seems to be falling for this enigmatic diner lady.

He very much looks forward to seeing her again.

Chapter 3: Jenny's Men

It's Halloween, and the diner seems to be almost empty and Jenny is dressed as Sweeney Todd. She thought it would be funny if someone was to order a pie but no one did.

The few who are dining, aren't really in the Halloween spirit as they are dressed as they usually would dress and eating their food in a sombre silence. It's like dining with the dead, she thinks.

Danny sits two tables away from the counter. Not too close but close enough to steal a glance at Jenny every now and again. He is dressed as a policeman; something he wanted to be when he was little but History – it seemed – was a safer option for him. He wasn't the most brave or strongest of men and he was okay with that. He didn't try to be.

He watches as she whizzes from this table to that, never once dropping the smile she's plastered on to keep the customers coming. He is transfixed with her, almost as if he was under a spell but he doesn't believe in witchcraft so he is certain; his feelings towards her are the real deal.

A cool breeze tickles his skin; as the door to the diner opens and a man makes his way inside. He is tall, dressed in all black and walking in a way that would suggest he was up to no good. He was shifty.

"Okay, love?"

He says.

Jenny jumps at his presence and spins on her heel to greet him but before any words escape her smiling mouth, the man has moved on and is making his way behind the counter.

Gathering he must work there, Danny stops eyeing him

suspiciously and turns his gaze back to Jenny. She is balancing three plates, a cup and a sauce bottle in her arms now and he almost feels compelled to get up and help her but he figures it's best not to. He doesn't want her to know he is watching her and so, he remains in his seat.

She places the plates on the counter and addresses the man behind it, who is now eating one of the cakes that sit; temptingly in a glass cabinet.

"I didn't know you were coming in today."

She says, with a flaccid tone.

"I was bored so thought, why not?"

He replies, shrugging his shoulders.

"Oh."

She says, and the man brushes the cake crumbs off of his shirt and moves closer to her.

"You're not happy to see me?"

He asks, almost a little hurt.

"No."

She shakes her head.

"I mean, yes! But, I just thought I would be alone today."

He grins.

"Secret boyfriend have you, love?"

Danny detects an air of nervousness around Jenny and before he can ponder why that is, the door bursts open and this time, in runs a little girl.

"Mommy! Mommy!"

She cries.

"Daddy said if I am as good as a cherub on a big, fluffy cloud, I can get some ice cream... and I've been good!"

The little girl runs to Jenny; who scoops her up in her arms, holding her more carefully than she did the plates. The man in black looks at her and smiles sheepishly.

"I see."

He says, catching on to the situation.

"didn't want me getting in the way, yeah?"

Jenny puts her little girl down and gives him an apologetic look in response. He doesn't seem to accept the apology and hastily clears the plates away.

She turns to her little girl.

"Where is your daddy, Dahlia?"

The little girl points outside to a man who looks much older than Jenny.

"He's outside. He's being a silly man."

Jenny smiles and waves for the man to come in and Danny tries not to be too obvious as he watches him, hesitantly make his way inside.

"I saw... you know?"

The older man says, nodding his head towards the man in black.

"I thought it was best if I wait outside."

He looks at his feet.

"Oh no, you're always welcome in here, big man, It's me that wasn't invited today. Wasn't it, Jennifer?"

The man in black stands between them now, creating a tension that was most uncomfortable, even to those who were just mere spectators.

"I didn't say that, James..."

She sighs.

"I Just-"

"She just thought she would be alone so, I will leave her to it."

He cuts in.

"Catch you later, Jennifer. See you around, Dahlia."

He ruffles the hair of the little girl and makes an exit, even more shifty than his entrance.

Jenny is about to speak but once again is interrupted. This

time by her little girl Dahlia, tugging on her apron.
"Daddy said I can have ice cream."
She whispers.
"Well, if daddy said you could and I have ice cream here then, why don't you jump up on the big girls stool and I'll get your favourite kind."
"Vanilla!"
The little girl sings.
"I know, sweetheart. Two minutes."

Danny sips his coffee slowly and watches as the older man also takes a seat. He wonders what attracted Jenny to him, what made her want to have a baby with him and what the man in black had to do with it all.

He tried not to think about it too much, knowing it was none of his business but like every person who had ever fallen for someone who wasn't available; he wondered, what did that man there have that he didn't?

"Freeze, this sticks up!"

His concentration is broken as he turns to see the little girl standing beside him, pointer fingers together to simulate a gun and she is pointing them inches from his face.

"Dahlia, you can't be scaring the customers like that."

Jenny says, throwing an apologetic look at Danny.

"Let this nice 'policeman', drink his coffee."

he almost forgot he was wearing a costume.

"It's okay."

He smiles at Jenny, who is now distracting Dahlia with the ice cream and she smiles back.

"She gets overexcited sometimes but she's harmless."

He turns his attention to the man speaking. Dahlia's dad. Jenny's man.

"So, how old is she?"

Danny didn't mean to ask this question in a tone that cried, "how long have you been with Jenny?" but the man didn't seem to pick up on it.

"She's 5. She will be six in July."

He says, smiling.

Danny didn't like this man's face. He hated that he was thinking this way but the man just looked too 'fatherly', he thinks and he imagines that would make him a good partner too. It was the eyes; they were kind and his lazy smile was just sickening to Danny. He forces a smile and pretends to be happy for them.

"Her mother-"

The man continues.

"Jen and I, we split when she was two years old."

This revelation catches Danny by surprise and suddenly, he's back in the game. Jenny is single.

"I'm sorry to hear that."

He lies, and the man smiles that sickening smile, at him again.

"So..."

Danny says, diving into the conversation, trying to get more information.

"you get her weekends or...?

"Oh, she lives with me."

The man replies.

"Yeah, Jen and James live in a small apartment and I have more room so... y'know."

Danny doesn't know. He would like to know more, starting with who James is but he has a suspicion that it's the man in black; the shifty guy. Jenny isn't single after all.

"I'm an old tomato".

Dahlia interjects once more and It doesn't take long for Danny to realise, she means 'ultimatum'.

He is confused as to what kind of ultimatum was in place

though; get shot of the boyfriend so the kid can stay with Jenny or keep the boyfriend and the kid goes with daddy, perhaps. It confused him even further when it dawned on him – if this was the case – she chose the latter. He couldn't see what was so great about the lanky man in black that would cancel out all the greatness that came with being a mother to a beautiful, little girl. He sips his coffee and observes Jenny some more. A puzzle he would never solve, he realises.

"Well, I like old tomatoes."

He says, lightening the mood and before he leaves, he spends one last thought on the man that he deemed shifty and determines; if Jenny couldn't even choose her own kid over him, what chance did he have with her?

Maybe he didn't want to be with someone who made such frivolous decisions anyway. He decides that, maybe it's best if he doesn't come back here.

He leaves.

Chapter 4: Locked Vault

It's Sunday afternoon – the day after Halloween – and James and Jenny are cuddled up on their sofa.

Jenny looks comfortable and content, while James looks like he is trying to piece something together in his mind.

He sighs.

"So what was all that about yesterday, Jennifer?"

He asks, finally.

"What's that?"

She wonders, not knowing what he is talking about.

"In the shop, with the kid. Why didn't you want me there?"

Jenny pulls away and gives him a confused look.

"I didn't say that I didn't want you there."

She huffs.

"No, you didn't."

He shifts away from her a little.

"But I could just tell you would rather that I wasn't, you know... there."

He looks hurt and her confusion turns to sympathy.

"It's just awkward, you know? You and William don't see eye to eye and -"

"But, I love Dahlia. I want to be a part of her life, Jennifer."

She takes his hand in reassurance, loving the way he never abbreviates her name.

"You are, James."

She says, slowly.

"I swear to God you are but you know what he is like."

James does know. He doesn't let on to just how much he

knows but he's not going to press her about this any further. He let's it drop.

He grins as he latches onto a new subject.

"I was thinking..."

He says, his eyes shining.

"If Dahlia was to be a flower girl..."

He searches for a reaction before continuing.

"What colour dress would she like?"

"Flower girl?"

Jenny asks, not really catching on.

"If we were to get married."

Jenny's tummy flips forward and back as she thinks about what that would mean.

On one hand, she would be promising to spend the rest of her life with the man she loves but on the other, she would have to tell William too and that's something, she doesn't see going down too well; not to mention, the secret she has been keeping for some time now. It's too messy.

"Are you asking me to marry you, James?"

She asks, unsure.

"I mean, you are being serious, right?"

James smiles bashfully.

"I might be."

He says, taking a deep breath.

"In fact, I might just have a ring in that little, blue box on the table."

She looks to the box he is referring to – wondering how long it's been sitting there, without her knowing – and she isn't quite sure what to do or say next. She just stares.

"You going to open it, or will I?"

He asks, smiling.

Jenny just nods and James reaches for the box and in one swift move, he gets down on bended knee.

In Her Shadow

"Jennifer..."

He lets out a little laugh.

"Aw, I feel a bit silly, you know."

He admits, shyly.

"I've never done this before and I've never really understood the whole down on one knee thing. It's just uncomfortable. But even if it were tradition to crawl across burning coals..."

He grins.

"At this point, I'd definitely do it."

He takes an even deeper breath and gently exhales.

"I'd do anything for you, you know that, love and I try to never ask anything of you in return but this time, I'm asking..."

He takes her hand.

"Jennifer, will you marry me? Please, marry me, Jennifer."

Her face stings as tears spill from her forest green eyes. She still can't find words.

"Don't cry, love. Please, don't cry."

James starts wiping away her tears.

"This is good. This is a happy thing, is it not?"

He pulls her close and plants a kiss atop her head. She clings to him, trembling and uncertain.

He doesn't detect the uncertainty but this isn't how he imagined this moment to go. He thought she'd smile her brightest smile and accept his proposal but instead, he just made her sad. He didn't like that.

"How can I make it better, love?"

He asks, feeling helpless.

"Tell me and I'll do what I can but please, don't cry."

She clings tighter and clears her throat.

"It's a nightmare, James."

She says, finally.

"It's all a nightmare."

He holds her tight, trying to unscramble the hidden meaning of those words but he needs more to go on.

"What's a nightmare, love? If it's nightmares you're having, I'll shoot the sandman who brought them to you."

He wipes away more of her tears.

"Tell me, why so sad?"

She tries to pull away but James won't let go. He cradles her and strokes her hair, trying to soothe her so speech will come easy.

"I have to tell you something, James but you have to promise not to tell anyone."

She takes a deep breath.

"Especially Dahlia, James."

She continues.

"She can't know."

He plants another kiss on her head and encourages her to continue; reassuring her that anything she says, is safe with him. He is a locked vault.

She struggles on.

"I'm sick."

Two words were all she could muster but they were said heavily, in a way that let James know, she didn't mean she just had a common cold or a twenty-four hour tummy bug.

He thought the worst because he knew, the worst was close at hand.

He too cries.

Chapter 5: Made Of Glass

It's Monday morning, a fresh new day and usually Jenny's alarm wakes her up at 6am, so she can get ready and be in the diner by 8:30am but today; the alarm doesn't sound off.

As her body is used to waking up on time, she rises anyway and finds that James isn't beside her. He's usually still lying there, arm over his head and clinging on to the last few minutes of his dreams.

She sits still. Wondering if maybe he left for the diner already or maybe – the most horrible thought enters her mind – he couldn't handle what she told him and he left her – for good – as she slept.

She pushes that thought to the back of her head as she hears footsteps in the kitchen and she gets up, pulls on her dressing gown and she goes to investigate.

Upon entering the kitchen, she is met with the sight of James in his boxers – and a t-shirt that she thinks might be hers – cleaning the oven.

She laughs, giving him a fright and when he spins around, she sees that the t-shirt is definitely hers.

"New shirt?"

He grins and leans against the kitchen counter.

"I've always thought women's clothing felt better against my skin, why is that?"

He asks, half serious.

"It's made by the hands of angels and approved by unicorns."

Jenny jokes.

"Oh, that makes sense."

He laughs.

"Come here, you!"

She rolls her eyes and he pulls her in for a kiss and a cuddle.

She snuggles into his shoulder and smiles softly. It's almost as if last night didn't happen, that he doesn't know she is sick and so he's not treating her that way; like she is made of glass and easy to break.

However, there was still the matter of the alarm that didn't go off.

"James, tell me this."

She starts.

"Why didn't the alarm go off this morning? I remember setting it."

He shrugs, pretending he doesn't know what she's trying to insinuate.

"Needs a new battery?"

She glares at him.

"Or..."

She says, hands on her hips.

"Someone just needs to not tamper with it."

He raises his hands in surrender.

"Sorry. I thought maybe you'd like the extra sleep."

He says, hesitating to continue.

"Maybe... you'd like to stay at home today?"

And there it is! The change, she thinks. Last night did happen and now she is his sick girlfriend, as opposed to just his girlfriend. About that, she had been thinking before she fell asleep and came to a final decision.

"Yes!"

She says enthusiastically.

"You're staying home?"

She shakes her head.

"No. I mean yes! Yes, I'll stay home, I'd like to rest but I mean yes..."

She grins.

"To the other thing."

James doesn't catch her meaning.

"You wanted the extra sleep?"

He asks, causing Jenny to sigh dramatically.

"I'll marry you, you madman!"

He drops his jaw in astonishment and Jenny smiles the smile, he so desperately wanted to see last night. He smiles back and throws his arms around her once more. This time, he squeezes tighter and this makes Jenny very happy as he sees, she is not made of glass and it's okay to hug her like he did before he knew, what he knows now.

"Jennifer, I can't believe it!"

He cries.

"You really are wicked, you know that?"

She rolls her eyes and takes a step back.

"To be fair, I didn't make you wait THAT long."

He nods.

"Even a mere millisecond is far too long to wait for such an answer but, it was worth the wait all the same."

He says, chewing on his lip.

"Thank you. A million times thank you! You've no idea what this means."

"That Dahlia gets to be a flower girl, after all?"

He pulls her close again.

"Aw, Jennifer! You'd actually let her?"

This means the world to him.

"Can we tell her when she's here at the weekend?"

Jenny pulls back. She never thought that far ahead and is stupendously overwhelmed. She keeps smiling.

"Baby steps, husband to be. Baby steps."

James dances around, as if his feet have just caught fire and he doesn't even attempt to mask his excitement or hide the tears of joy that are forming in his big, brown eyes. He's the happiest he has ever been.

Jenny's heart fills with magic, as she watches him – almost pixie like – fill and fill with a happy energy; she hasn't seen before.

"So... I get the day off?"

She asks, bringing him back to the room.

His dancing comes to an end as he remembers his plans for today.

"Yes."

He nods.

"Yes, you get to do whatever you wish and I get to go to the diner and be you for the day."

She looks him up and down.

"Ah, that explains the shirt."

He chuckles.

"Sorry, love. It was closest thing to me."

He smooths his hands over it.

"I've probably stretched it out, haven't I? I'll get you a new one, I promise"

She rolls her eyes and heads to the living room. James follows.

"Do you want something to eat, love?"

He asks.

"I have time to make breakfast before I get ready."

Jenny feels down the side of the sofa and retrieves a chocolate bar.

"Nope."

She starts to unwrap it.

"I'm going to eat this and catch up on some shows."

James laughs.

In Her Shadow

"I knew you had a secret stash!"

He goes to get ready, while Jenny gets started on her shows and when he returns; he has a more stony expression on his face.

"Sweetheart..."

He nervously tugs at the bottom of his shirt.

"Last night, you know-"

"Don't want to talk about it, James."

"But -"

Jenny throws her hands up in protest. She really didn't want to discuss this but James had to know more.

"How long?"

He asks quickly.

"How long what?"

She replies.

A cold atmosphere suddenly floods into the room as James is too afraid to hear the answer and Jenny realizes he is asking, how long she has left to live.

"You will be late if you don't leave now."

She says, trying to avoid answering.

"I just need to know."

He sighs.

"Does it matter?"

James thinks about this. of course, it does matter. He wants to know how much longer he gets to have the love of his life, be the love of his life but also; a new thought niggles in his mind.

"Well..."

He clears his throat.

"You will marry me, won't you?"

Jenny huffs.

"I said I would, didn't I?"

He bites his lip.

"When?"

He asks, thinking that'll give him some kind of answer to his other question too.

"Soon..."

He nods and accepts the answer, not wanting to push her further as she said she doesn't want to talk about it.

He blows her a kiss and heads straight to the diner.

He's cleaning the counter, whistling as he does so and doesn't notice he has a customer waiting to be served. That customer is Danny.

He clears his throat to get attention and when James sees him, he tries to hide his annoyance at his presence. He had previously noticed the way that he looks at Jenny, trying to hide that he's not watching her but really; he soaked up her every move and It made James uncomfortable.

"You can't keep away, can you?"

He jokes.

"What can I get for ya?"

"Coffee. Milk, no sugar."

James is about to turn away when Danny takes hold of his arm.

"Why do you wear all that black?"

Out of all the questions he had for James, this was the one he hadn't intended on asking but it was too late to take it back.

"Beg your pardon?"

Laughs James and pulls his arm away.

"You. You walk around here like you're trying to be Joey Ramone or something. What's the deal with that?"

James smirks. It's not the first time he has been spoken to this way but for the first time, he keeps a cool head.

"Why do you order your coffee with milk but no sugar?"

He asks, looking him up and down.

In Her Shadow

"I don't like my coffee with sugar."

Danny replies, shrugging his shoulders.

"Well, officer, I don't like my clothing with bright colours."

Danny tuts.

"I'll have the usual."

James rolls his eyes. The kid hadn't been to the diner a handful of times and already he's having, 'the usual', he thinks.

"Right then..."

He says, and goes to make the 'milk, no sugar' coffee.

Danny slumps down in one of the counter seats and watches him closely. He's decided, he's definitely shifty and there was just something about him that wasn't right. He wanted to know what.

James places the coffee in front of him and shakes his head when he tries to pay.

"This one is on me."

He says, trying to be friendly.

"No, I want to pay."

"Suit yourself. I was just trying to be nice, mate."

"We aren't mates."

Danny slams the money down on the counter, not aware of the tone he is taking with James and goes to sip his coffee.

James pulls it away.

"You have a problem with me?"

He asks, locking eyes with him.

Danny is affronted but doesn't reach to take the coffee back.

"What makes you think that?"

"Joey Ramone?"

Danny smirks.

"Well, I just think you're a bit of a poser is all and can't figure out what Jenny sees in you."

James gets it now. This guy had quite clearly developed a

little crush on Jenny and was taking it out on him.
    He shrugs his shoulders.
    "Why don't you ask Jennifer what she sees."
    He says, still holding onto the coffee.
    "I would but she's not here."
    Danny leans in.
    "Your doing?"
    He asks.
    "Meaning?"
    James wonders.
    "Did you see her get a little friendly with me and feel threatened? Maybe forced her to stay home?"
    James stares at him in disbelief and wonders if he knows that he is actually saying this stuff out loud – to James' face – and not just thinking it.
    "First."
    He says, matter-of-factly.
    "I don't force Jennifer to do anything and second, she's a very friendly person."
    He takes hold of Danny's shoulder and leans in.
    "It's not just you, mate."
    He whispers.
    "Told you, I'm not your mate."
    Danny snaps, brushing James' hand away.
    "And again, I wonder, what's your problem?"
    Danny suddenly becomes aware of his surroundings and he doesn't like the way he acted like a petulant child because James had Jenny and he didn't. He wasn't one for apologies though.
    "You called me 'officer', why?"
    James shrugs.
    "That's what you were dressed as on Halloween and I don't know your name."

In Her Shadow

This wounds Danny, slightly. A revelation that Jenny doesn't even talk about him.

"My name is Danny and I'm a History teacher."

He says, all pouty.

"Sorry, history teacher's anonymous was last week."

Smirks James.

Maybe that was it. Maybe Jenny liked his sense of humour but Danny knew he could be funny too.

"Oh, that's right."

He says.

"It's 'morons anonymous' this week. My mistake."

"Yeah, are you the only member of that group? Haven't seen any others today."

James smiles smugly and Danny is silenced. He thinks about throwing back, 'so you haven't looked in the mirror today?' but he knows this conversation is just ridiculous and petty and he won't be indulging in it further.

James senses this and he too, feels foolish.

"I'll make you a fresh coffee."

He says, drawing a line under the conversation.

Both men sit in an awkward silence. Not wanting to start a new dialogue with each other because, not only are they stubborn but they have both decided; that the other is an idiot and won't be wasting any more energy there.

The door to the diner swings open and Danny turns in his seat to see Jenny's ex William, sauntering in as if he owns the place and looking much more confident – almost full of himself – than he did, when he was in previously.

James looks up and this time, doesn't try to hide that he is annoyed by the man on the other side of the counter. He really doesn't want him there.

"What do you want?"

William nudges Danny.

"You know, he's just so charming, isn't he?"

Danny doesn't respond. This has nothing to do with him but still, he will latch on to every word and see if there is anything he can use for leverage later on. Maybe they will act differently, with Jenny not around to bring out their best sides. He relishes the thought.

"Where's Jen?"

"Not here."

"Evidently. Where can I find her?"

"Why are you looking for her?"

William grows irritated and places his palms on the counter, leaning closer to James.

"We have a child together, I think that's reason enough."

James drops his attitude and adopts a look of concern.

"Is there something wrong with Dahlia?"

He asks, genuinely caring to know.

"It's nothing to do with you if there is."

James takes a deep breath.

"You know, I really care about that little girl. I'm not her daddy but I'm going to marry her mum and that has to count for something, surely?"

This slip of the tongue causes both William and Danny to drop their jaws and James mentally scolds himself, knowing he shouldn't have let it slip out like that but, the damage was done.

"She - she can't marry you."

William stutters.

"Why can't she, mate?"

Asks James.

Danny pounds his fist against the counter.

"Don't you hate that? Don't you hate when he calls you that and in that stupid, English accent of his?"

Both men look at him, as if they forgot he was even there

and he wishes the ground would just swallow him up, where he sat. He shrinks into the seat, trying to take up as little space as possible and continues to just watch.

James sighs.

"Will, Listen..."

He says, trying to bring the situation to a calm.

"I didn't-"

"You did!

William snaps.

"You were probably dying to call me during the proposal, so I could hear her answer!"

He scowls at James.

"When did you ask her?"

James shakes his head, trying to keep his cool and comes round to the other side of the counter; placing himself just inches from William.

"Wasn't like that at all."

He says, stuffing his hands in his pockets.

"I only asked her last night and she only gave me her answer this morning."

William runs his hand through his hair, looking more menacing than he probably intended to show.

"Where is she?"

He asks again.

"Look, just leave her today, eh?"

They stare each other down, as if they have just stepped into the 'old west' and are about to draw their pistols.

"What if Dahlia was sick?"

"Is she?"

"No. But, what if she was and you're keeping me from fetching her mother?"

James grunts.

"She's not a Frisbee, mate and there are these things

called... what is it again, Dan? A phone?"

Danny still doesn't open his mouth and William doesn't appreciate James' sarcasm. He desperately wants to see Jenny but his reason for wanting to see her in the first place has changed, in the last few seconds.

He originally wanted to discuss a day trip. Where he, Dahlia and Jenny could spend some time as a family but now, he wants to see her to change her mind about marrying James.

"It's an urgent matter all the same."

He says, bringing his voice down to a serious tone.

"Something that needs to be done face to face."

James narrows his eyes.

"You see, the problem with that, Will."

He says, switching his hands from pockets to hips.

"I'm standing face to face with you now and you look like a rabid dog, that's just about to rip out my jugular. So it begs the question; why would I let you, you know..."

He flips his hands towards William and back to him.

"'Face to face' with Jennifer?"

William collects himself, realising the state he is getting himself into and takes a seat.

James returns to his position behind the counter.

"Coffee?"

He offers.

"No. Just tell me where she is..."

He braces himself.

"Please?"

This 'please' tasted bitter on William's tongue but he thought in saying it, he would get what he wanted. James ignores it and goes to make him a coffee anyway.

Danny, having finished his coffee, is now writing something on a napkin. He finishes, stealthily slides the napkin to William and leaves.

In Her Shadow

The napkin reads, 'I think he beats her.'

William scrunches the napkin up and stuffs it in his pocket; unsure of what to make of it but before he can contemplate it further, a coffee – in a 'to go' cup - is placed in front of him.

"Get the hint?"

James asks, pointedly.

"I do"

William replies.

"But before I go, why isn't she here today anyway?"

"Jennifer isn't here because she deserves the rest."

James says.

"So, she's at yours?"

"She's at ours, yes."

William picks up the cup and is ready to leave when James grabs his arm.

"I'm warning you, Will. Leave her alone today."

He snatches his arm away and leans forward so he can whisper and be heard clearly.

"Why?"

He asks, with a grin.

"Why today? Don't want me to see what you have done to her, is that it?"

Before James can ask what he means by that statement, William is already scurrying towards the exit. Before he leaves, he dumps the cup of coffee into the bin that sits there and continues, making his way to Jenny.

Chapter 6: Poor, Old Daddy

Jenny is lying on her sofa, half watching the TV and half thinking about how long she will get to to spend being, Mrs James Baker. Jenny Baker, wife of James Baker, mother of Dahlia Myers.

She never had to explain to anyone before that James wasn't Dahlia's dad. People always tended to assume he was or they knew William and didn't know that they were divorced now, so the topic never came up and they managed to keep up the illusion of 'happy families'; at parents evening's and the like.

She wonders if this – marrying James – will change people's opinions of her. Wonders if it will make them think that she was unfaithful, when that wasn't the case.

Their relationship didn't end because of infidelity. Jenny had fallen out of love with William. He wasn't the best husband but she still likes the part of him that is a great dad to Dahlia; so she tries to focus on that part, instead of the rest.

She turns her attention back to the TV but is interrupted with the sound of the door, being knocked on loudly and repeatedly.

She checks the spy-hole and sees William, standing there and muttering to himself. She opens the door and he bursts inside.

"Don't do it!"

He shouts, as he elbows her out of the way.

Jenny closes the door behind him and follows, cautiously; as he makes his way up the hall and to the living room.

"What's wrong, William?"

She asks, fearing that something bad has happened. .

"Is Dahlia okay?"

He throws himself onto the sofa and Jenny sits in the armchair across from him.

She is a little frightened by his manner.

"She's fine."

He tuts.

"Did you not hear me? I said, don't do it."

Jenny grips the arms of the chair.

"Don't do what?"

She asks, unaware that he has just been at the diner and James has filled him in, on their plan to marry.

"Marry that idiot!"

She gasps, and her thoughts start to race at a million miles a minute as she wonders; how much he actually knows. Did he know about her being 'sick' too, she panics.

"William, I don't-"

"He told me."

William says, not letting her finish..

"Well, he let it slip but the point is, I know."

Jenny takes a deep breath and clears her throat. She figures that, he must only know about the proposal part and she feels more at ease.

"You weren't supposed to find out like that. We were-"

"See!"

He cries.

"He's no good, he's failing you already!"

"And you are good?!"

She didn't mean to snap but she promised herself, she would never let anyone – no matter who they were – say a bad word about James.

William jumps from the sofa, frightening her even more

and throws himself to his knees; at her feet.

"This isn't about me, Jen."

He sighs, heavily.

"It's him. There's something not right about him."

Jenny tuts.

"You don't even know him, William."

"I don't want to know him."

He really didn't anticipate that James was going to be around this long. He thought he and Jenny would somehow work things out and get back together but; he was still there, in Jenny's bed and playing dad to his daughter. He didn't like it one bit.

"And more to the point."

He says, calmly.

"I don't want Dahlia to know him either."

This last statement angers Jenny.

"Dahlia loves the bones of him, William."

She says, and he sneers at her. He hates when she uses phrases like that, phrases that James has taught her.

"She doesn't share your ignorance."

She adds, when she sees the look in his eye.

William changes his position so that he is sitting with his legs in a basket and his head in his hands. He is trying to project a sense of vulnerability; hoping that Jenny will fall for it and throw her arms around him, at least.

This isn't the first time she has seen him in this particular state though and so, this time; she doesn't sympathize or feel guilty. She is much stronger than that now.

"I want you to leave,"

She says, quietly.

"You don't belong here, William."

She is surprised to hear sobs coming from him – a new tactic, she thinks – but she is still not moved enough, to take

In Her Shadow

pity on him.

"One chance, Jen."

He whispers, trying to sound as pitiful as he can.

"One last chance, please. That's all I'm asking."

"That's all you ever ask."

She says, rolling her eyes.

"If I were to give you that chance – which I wouldn't – it would probably amount to more than a hundred, one, last chances."

"It's different this time."

He argues, looking up at her.

"I promise you. I wo-"

"It's always different, William. Different day, different house, different change of clothes but still; it's the same, old you that's wearing them."

Never one to talk back to him before, Jenny is silently proud of herself as she doesn't waver in her response.

He doesn't move.

"You're right."

He sighs, making his way back onto his knees.

"I'm not going to argue but this time-"

"I love James, William."

She says, shutting him down..

"I am going to marry him and I'm going to do it soon."

William stands. His face is contorted in anger and before Jenny can stand too, he lunges and traps her in the chair; keeping his hands gripped steady on each of the arm rests.

"I told you before, if you don't leave him; Dahlia stays with me. I guess she's not enough for you but we will see how much she means to you when you marry him."

He says, bringing his face a little closer to hers.

"Because – and mark my words, Jen – you do that, and you will never see her again!"

He releases her but she doesn't move. Instead, tears trickle down her face and she tries to pull herself together but to no avail. She isn't as strong as she thought, it seems.

William doesn't say another word. He exits, slamming every door he walks through and Jenny sits shaken.

She remains still and silent for what feels like hours but is only ten minutes, when she hears the front door open.

Afraid it may be William again, she jumps out of her seat and takes on a stance of defence. Her defences melt when she sees that it's James and she throws herself into his arms.

"There, there, love."

He soothes, kissing her cheeks.

"Let's sit down and we can talk about it."

He leads her to the sofa and gently pulls her down close to him. She clings to his arm tight and he clenches his jaw, even tighter. He knows instantly that William didn't heed his warning.

"Did he hurt you?"

She shakes her head fiercely and let's out gentle sobs.

"What did he do?"

He asks, trying to remain calm.

"He- he-"

She starts, but struggles to continue so James strokes her hair and squeezes her hand until she is ready.

She breathes in and then out, in and then out and brings herself to a calm.

"He said, if I marry you-"

"Jennifer, I am so sorry, it just slipped out. I wasn't think-"

"I won't see Dahlia again."

He grinds his teeth. This is the straw that has not only broken the camels back, but sucked every ounce of patience from it too.

"He can't do that."

He says, shaking his head.

"Trust me, Jennifer, he can't do that."

Jenny does trust him and this was all he had to say to ease her mind. She knew that alone, she wouldn't have the strength to fight William but with James by her side, she could move – even lift – mountains.

He wouldn't let her down.

Later that night, when they retire to bed; James waits for Jenny to fall asleep before he sneaks out and drives to William's place.

He doesn't have a stellar plan but he knows he wants to tell him that what he did today, was not okay. He needed to know that, he won't get away with it.

He pulls up outside the house and sends a text to him, telling him to come outside and have a chat in the car. William doesn't respond, leaving James with no choice but to knock on the door.

William answers and pulls the door shut behind him and steps out on to the path with James.

"What are you doing here?"

He demands, and James smirks.

"Like you don't know."

He says, through gritted teeth.

"Like you thought I'd just let you scare Jennifer and do nothing."

William places his hands firmly on his hips.

"I don't know what you're talking about."

He says, playing dumb.

"Oh, don't play that game with me, mate."

James warns him.

"You know fine well wha-"

"So, what?"

William snorts.

"You here to rough me up a bit, tell Jen I won't be bothering her again because you've left me with a nice ring around my eye?"

James bites his lip and shakes his head.

"You'd like that, wouldn't you?"

He says, moving towards him.

"Poor, old daddy. Never did anything wrong and yet, his face is bruised and his bones are broken. Can't be letting a child live with someone like that, no."

"So..."

says William, stepping forward and eyeing James from heel to head.

"Which bone are you going to attempt to break first?"

He throws his fists up, ready for an attack but James doesn't even flinch.

"I'm not here to roll around with you, Will – as much as you'd probably like that – I'm just here to let you know; if you get Jennifer in that state again, there will be consequences."

William chuckles.

"Oh, I'm terrified."

He says, dropping his hands.

"You will be."

James threatens.

Once again, they stare each other down.

"I'll never be afraid of you, James."

William says, with a smile.

"You're nothing and she will see that, you know."

James grins.

"And yet, she's wearing my ring. While yours is where?"

He taunts.

"Oh, that's right, she gave it back to you."

William grabs him by the shoulders and brings his face close to his. James laughs and pushes him away, knocking him

In Her Shadow

against his front door. The door opens, to reveal Dahlia; staring wide eyed.

Neither men notice her as they face off once more.

"James, you're only making things worse for Jen."

"No! You are!"

James throws back.

"You have absolutely no idea what the girl is going through."

He is frustrated. He wants him to know exactly what is going on but that would mean, betraying Jenny. She didn't want anyone to know.

"What you're putting her through, more like."

William replies.

"You're the one that wants to stop her from seeing her daughter."

"Yes and with good reason."

James laughs.

"What, 'cause she's found someone new? Hardly a good reason, mate."

He closes his eyes and tries to keep his temper from rising.

He knows that this is a big part of the problem, that William can't stand that Jenny has moved on but; he wont be stepping into William's shoes and trying to see things from his point of view. There was much more to it than that and this wasn't the time nor the place, to get into it. He calms down.

"I don't want to fight with you, Will."

He sighs, opening his eyes and locking them on William's.

"I'm asking nicely. Please, don't do that do her."

William mocks James' accent.

"Please don't do that to her. God, how can she stand you and that whiny voice?"

Letting his temper finally get the better of him; James

throws a punch, hitting William on the jaw and before he can throw another, he hears a scream.

Dahlia runs towards her dad and James drops his hands to his side, in horror.

"Dahlia, sweetheart... no... you're supposed to be in your bed."

He turns to William.

"She's supposed to be in her bed, Will..."

He crouches down to her level to apologise and hug her but she clings on to William and pulls away from James.

William takes her hand and leads her back inside.

"I think you should leave now."

He glares at James.

"I will be seeing you tomorrow."

James is deflated as he heads to his car and just sits behind the wheel in a daze. He can't quite believe that he raised his hands at all, never mind Dahlia seeing him do it.

He feels he has let Jenny down and when he finally finds the strength to drive and return home; he tiptoes inside and takes his place beside her. He doesn't sleep. He watches as she dreams and wonders if she could ever forgive him. He knows William will run to tell her everything so he thinks it best, if he tells her himself in the morning.

He really didn't want her to start her day that way though.

Chapter 7: The Vault Opens

"Morning, love. How did you sleep?"

James plants a kiss on Jenny's forehead and she smiles as she breathes in his scent.

He always smelled of leather and petrol. A perfume that she had grown to love as it reminded her of the nights she would shiver and he – always the gentleman – would let her wear his favourite leather jacket and on the days she was most anxious; he would give her his petrol lighter as the sound of the 'click, clunk' as she opened and closed it, soothed her.

He was a dream, she thought.

"Yeah, fine. How come you didn't sleep?"

She asks, getting ready to read his face.

James hovers in his tracks for a minute, unsure of how to tell her and before he opens his mouth; she strokes his cheek and smiles.

"It's okay, I know."

He covers her hand with his and rests into her touch.

"He got there first, eh?"

"He sent me a very lengthy text, before you even got home."

He pulls away.

"I'm really sorry, Jennifer. I was just so mad and I know that's no excuse but, I couldn't stop myself."

"It's okay."

She squeezes his arm.

"It's really not."

He sighs.

"No, it's not okay that Dahlia saw. She really should have been sleeping but turns out, he let her stay up to watch some cartoons and that isn't your fault."

His heart sinks.

"Does she hate me?"

He's afraid to hear the answer as, Dahlia means the world to him..

"Does she think I am a bad man?"

Jenny shakes her head.

"She won't think that forever, don't worry."

He does worry. His sole intention was to let William know he couldn't keep Dahlia from Jenny and now, he has even more motive to do just that. He messed up. Big time, he thinks.

"If you'd like to take the day again, love."

He says, pulling himself together.

"I don't mind going to the diner."

She smiles.

"Nope. I feel good and to be honest, I kinda missed it when I wasn't there yesterday."

She takes his hand.

"You can always come by in the afternoon, if you want. Give me some company?"

James laughs.

"I think that Danny guy will be there to keep you company..."

Jenny racks her brain.

"Danny?"

She asks, not knowing who he is meaning.

"The guy who sits close to the counter, watching your every move. Think he has a crush on you, you know."

She snaps her fingers as she remembers.

"Oh! Milk and no sugar guy."

She pictures him sitting there.

"He's just a kid!"

"He's a history teacher, you know. Probably around the same age as you."

James teases.

"He looks about 20."

She replies.

"And? You're 26, love."

She giggles.

"Jealous? Afraid I'll run away with him?"

James tickles her.

"Well, I dunno, do I?"

He jokes.

"Maybe you're going off the older men. I mean, I'm 38, Will is 46..."

He doesn't continue. He didn't mean to bring him into the conversation when they were having a light, happy moment.

He changes the subject.

"Right!"

He says, dropping his arms by his sides.

"I'll swing by later but I have a few things to do first and then, I'm all yours."

She hugs him tightly.

"I dunno, baby..."

She looks up at him, with a mischievous smile.

"A history teacher, you say?"

He pulls away and rolls his eyes.

"Better not keep him waiting, love. See you soon."

With that, she skips out the door and James texts William, telling him to come around as he said he would be seeing James today and he wanted to get it over with and do so, while Jenny wasn't there.

William arrives fifteen minutes later and walks right in, past

James and on to the living room.

James follows.

They both sit on opposite ends of the room; William on the sofa and James in the armchair. The tension between the two is so strong, you would need a sledgehammer to smash through it.

William tuts.

"Look, you asked me to come here so, what do you want?"

James clasps his hands in his lap.

"You said you would see me today so, I gave you the opportunity."

He says, sitting back.

"What do you want to see me about?"

William blinks in amazement. He can't believe just how nonchalant James is being about it all. It really bugged him.

"Well, you hit me and-"

"I know, I was there. Next part."

William clenches his jaw.

"I hope you know, you'll never get a chance to do that again. I know you probably get away with it with Jen but-"

James jumps to his feet.

"What?!"

He demands.

"What part?"

William asks, enjoying the fact that he's caught him off guard.

"Getting away with it with Jennifer?"

James says, smoothing his hands over his shirt and then locking them, firmly on his hips.

"Explain."

William reaches into his pocket and pulls out the crumpled up napkin, with Danny's writing on it.

"This."

He says, holding it out to him.

James snatches it from him and reads, still not making sense of what his point his.

"You think who beats who?"

He asks, confused.

"Oh, not me. I didn't write that."

William smiles smugly.

"It was given to me."

The penny finally drops as James realizes that it was written about him. He sits back down.

"Who gave you it?"

He asks, trying to wrap his head around the words on the napkin.

"Is it true?"

William wonders.

"Of course it's not! Who wrote it?"

"It doesn't matter who wrote it. Again, is it true?"

"I told you, no, it's not true."

"Why would he write that and pass it specifically to me?"

James clenches his jaw.

"Again, who?"

He asks, wanting to throttle the person who wrote such a thing about him.

William shakes his head and James doesn't need to ask again because he has worked it out. It must have been Danny, who he has already determined; has a crush on Jenny.

"The kid at the diner, right?"

He grunts.

"The little, scrawny looking one who looks like he's just out of nappies?"

William nods and smiles a smile that reads sinister.

"You're caught out now."

He says, revelling in the moment.

James stands and leaves the room. When he returns, he has a glass in one hand and a bottle of fruit juice in the other.

He sits, appearing more relaxed than he was before and places the glass and the bottle on the coffee table; which sits between them both.

"So..."

He starts.

"What exactly is it I have been 'caught out' on, Will? Enlighten me."

William relaxes too, sinking into the sofa.

"That punch you threw my way last night."

He rubs his jaw.

"How many of those have landed on Jen?"

James is seething. He can't believe the audacity of William but somehow, he manages to remain in his seat and not leap at him.

"I've never so much as raised my voice at her, never mind my fists."

He says, his face straight and his voice steady.

"But I don't need to prove myself to - to the likes of you."

William scowls.

"Oh, but you do."

He leans forward.

"This is the mother of my child we are talking about."

James raises his hand, stopping him from continuing.

He didn't want to have this conversation today. He hadn't planned what he was going to say but he won't be made out a monster; when the real monster was sitting right in front of him.

"Shall I tell you about the first time we – Jennifer and I – were about to make love?"

He asks, as if he were chatting with an old friend.

"Excuse me?"

In Her Shadow

William is taken aback by the sudden shift in conversation but James continues.

"It wasn't the way it should have be-"

"I don't want to hear this, that's my wife!"

"Ex wife."

James reminds him, bringing his voice to a more serious tone. This certainly isn't an old friend sitting before him. This man isn't someone that James would ever consider a friend so, he wants William to be squirming in his seat; when the conversation is over.

"She's your ex wife, Will. Now let me finish, it's relevant to your accusation."

William's jaw tightens and he gives James a look that would be intended to kill him, if looks possessed such a power and although he doesn't want to hear this; he is curious to what the point is and so – begrudgingly – lets him continue.

"Don't worry, mate."

Says James, enjoying the fact that; the table is about to turn.

"I'm not going to go into detail. All you need to know is that, when I unbuttoned Jennifer's shirt and my eyes took in her bare skin for the first time? It didn't ignite passion in me."

Confusion colours William's face as he can't seem to grasp how any of this is relevant to the topic, he brought to the table.

"So, what?"

He asks, with a scowl on his face.

"Did she repel you, you not used to girls with a little more meat on their bones? Is that why she went and lost all that weight?"

James smirks as he picks up the glass he set down earlier.

"I was filled with horror. Disgust even."

He opens the bottle of fruit juice and pours some in the glass, until it is half full.

William watches him, waiting for him to continue and before James goes on; he places the glass back on top of the table, not drinking from it.

"Understand..."

He continues, eyes locked on William's eyes.

"There was nothing wrong with her body."

He smiles.

"I found her – and still do find her – incredibly beautiful. It was the markings that put me off."

"Markings?"

William doesn't pick up on where this is going.

"Bruises, to be precise. Big, black and blue and red bruises."

William gets it now, and James can almost see the excuses as they form in his mind, but never quite roll off the tip of his tongue; and he nods his head, as he confirms what he already knew.

"You did it."

He states.

"You put them there."

"She's lying!"

William snaps.

"I would never hurt her."

"She?"

"Jen. I would nev-"

"Yes, you said that part already and Jennifer, never even told me how they got there."

James hated the fact that she had an excuse for each and every bruise left on her body but now, he knows for sure that he was right. William had indeed hurt her and he will never get to do that again. He won't let him.

"She just put her shirt back on and left."

He adds, finishing his story.

Both men fall silent for a moment; James because he doesn't need to say more and William because he knows, he has been found out.

He is the first to break, in an attempt to defend himself.

"It's not like... it's not..."

James leans forward and pushes the glass towards him.

"Truth is hard to swallow, isn't it?"

William nods, as a squeezed out little tear; runs from both eyes.

James has no sympathy for him. In fact, he hasn't finished speaking, he decides.

"Now, you tell me."

He says, taking back the attention.

"Why am I – someone who never has and never will hurt Jennifer – wrong for her? Eh?"

He doesn't get a reply and a boiling anger starts to rise within him but he doesn't let it erupt.

"You know, that little twit in the diner asked what Jennifer saw in me too and I told him to ask her. Not because I wanted him to be put in his place but because, I myself, was unsure."

He licks his lips before continuing.

"I get it now though, I do. I'm her shadow."

William wipes his face.

"Her Shadow?"

He asks, thankful for any change of subject.

"It's what she calls me."

James replies.

"Why?"

"Because she said when I am around, that means there is light and shadows can only be found where there is light."

James leans forward.

"In her dark days, I bring light to her. You see?"

Tears spill from his eyes – tears that he didn't have to squeeze out – and he looks to William, who is suddenly filled with guilt.

"I do."

William sighs.

"No you don't."

James sniffs.

"You still think she's better off without me and maybe she is but; Will, mate, isn't that her decision?"

He bites his lip.

"Don't take Dahlia away from her. That little girl is more than a shadow. She's the Olympic flame and if Jennifer doesn't get to see her, the light that I bring? It won't be enough. It'll do her in."

William doesn't want to listen to this.

"Why has she never tried to fight me for her?"

He asks, not realising how stupid he sounds.

This question takes James by surprise. He thought William would know why, or at least; half of the reason why.

"Maybe she's afraid you will fight back with your fists."

His mind starts to wander, and the images he is conjuring up now; block everything else out.

"Or maybe she believes Dahlia is better with you, terrified that..."

He stops. He doesn't want to talk about what he is seeing now; it sends shivers straight up his spine.

"Terrified of what?"

William asks, snapping James out of his trance.

"Look, I've said too much as it is."

James really can't help himself. He has always been quite the impulsive person and he acts without thinking; and lets things slip out too easily.

"Drop it, okay?"

He sighs, and William doesn't want to.

"No. I need to know."

He urges.

James shakes his head but it's just too much to hold in and so, he decides to release it.

"Maybe she doesn't want Dahlia to find her; lying, cold and her lips all blue."

He regrets this slip of the tongue instantly.

"Meaning?"

William asks, not sure what James is trying to reveal to him.

James wipes his face.

"Meaning, she's dying."

He whispers, and despite regretting his previous statement; he had to make it clear. Jenny is dying.

"There, I said it. I'm not perfect, I've let her down yet again."

He throws his head in his hands.

"I'm not perfect..."

Silence surrounds them once again, this time it lingers longer.

The colour has drained from both their faces and their eyes are bloodshot. This is heavy.

"If it's any consolation..."

Says William, speaking first.

"I never thought you were perfect."

They laugh. Unexpectedly, and for the first time; they don't want to strangle each other.

This is something that rocks them both for, they are both in love with Jenny and in spite of their sins against her; they would take her place if they could.

"She didn't want you to tell anyone, did she?"

William asks, knowing how Jenny is good at keeping things to herself, never giving much away.

"No."

James shakes his head.

"I won't tell her you told me."

"It's fine. I don't keep secrets from Jennifer so, I'll tell her anyway."

William nods solemnly. Another thing that James is better at than him – telling the truth – and although it pained him to think it; he admired him for that.

"If you want..."

He says, not really wanting to do this but, he feels he needs to now.

"I can drop Dahlia off tomorrow. Here."

James sighs. Of course that's what he wants – what Jenny wants too – but he is still consumed with the guilt, from Dahlia witnessing him hit her father.

"Will she be okay with me?"

He asks, his heart heavy.

"I told her we were wrestling."

William replies, getting to his feet.

"Like they do on TV. She's none the wiser."

This leaves James delighted and as he watches William leave, he feels a massive weight has been lifted. Not just because they will try to be civil with one another now but because, he didn't have to go through this alone. Or so he thinks.

He remembers he told Jenny he would drop in at the diner to keep her company so, he heads there and once he arrives; he is greeted with the widest smile that melts his heart and has his knees knocking together.

"There he is, my shadow!"

Jenny sings.

He strides towards her, grinning from ear to ear and ducks under the counter to give her a tight hug.

In Her Shadow

"Sorry I'm late, love."

He says.

"It's okay.

She replies, and motions to some of the tables.

"We aren't rushed off our feet anyway."

James looks around, seeing that there aren't many people in but he isn't surprised that the seat – closest to the counter – is filled by Danny.

"Okay, Danny boy?"

He says, with a wink.

Danny pretends not to hear him. He doesn't want to act nice to him in front of Jenny and sips his coffee, while looking the other way.

James leans in and kisses Jenny on the cheek so he can whisper to her.

"So, he not asked you to run away with him yet?"

She giggles and shoves him playfully.

"Still waiting."

She jokes.

"Oh!"

James says, smiling.

"I've got something to tell you, love."

"Oh yeah, what's that?"

She raises her eyebrow at him.

"I have managed to get us a date with a very special, little lady tomorrow and I wondered; where would you like to go?"

Danny listens in and rolls his eyes. He grows to despise James more and more every day. The way he walked, his accent, the smarmy looks he gives him and the way Jenny goes all Bambi eyed whenever he is near.

"Hmm... to the moon?"

She breathes.

James chuckles.

"I'd love to but I don't think we have the proper shoes, love."

He would take her to the moon if he could, of course but he has a lovely – more realistic – plan. He would like to do something that would create a nice, family memory. He didn't get to have many of those when he was younger so, he wants Dahlia to get all those kinds of memories; while she can.

"How about a picnic in that big, fancy park?"

She kisses him.

"I suppose the moon can wait."

She says, loving his idea.

"So tell me, how much did you have to pay to get this little lady to join us?"

She asks, and James leans in to whisper once more.

"You do know I'm talking about Dahlia, right?"

She starts giggling.

"James, don't be gross!"

She says, shoving him again.

"Seriously, what's the catch?"

"No catch."

He shrugs his shoulders.

"None?"

She isn't convinced.

"He's just going to let us have her on a weekday?"

James tucks her hair behind her ears and plants a kiss on both of her cheeks.

"Thing is, love."

He tugs on the bottom of her shirt.

"You carried that little girl with you, in here."

He tickles her tummy.

"For nine months."

Jenny takes hold of his hand.

"If you want her with you, who is he to stop you? You're

her home."

She falls silent. She has never thought about it like that before and now she feels bad that she hasn't fought harder for Dahlia. James was right, she had as much right to have her as William did.

"Love?"

"I have customers to serve."

She steps away from him.

"Would it be okay if I asked you to go out and get some of Dahlia's favourite things, for our picnic?"

He nods. Jenny didn't have to tell James what to get as, he took interest in Dahlia; as if she were his own little girl and he knew, what she liked and what she didn't. She was also very similar to her mother and so, it wasn't the toughest job in the world, to make her smile.

"Of course. Whatever you need, love."

She whizzes away to serve her customers before he can ask if she is okay and he takes this opportunity, to approach Danny.

"You know napkins aren't for writing false information on, right?"

He says, towering over him.

"They're for wiping things like; spilled milk, sauce... blood."

The last word catches Danny off guard.

"Are you threatening me?"

He asks, shocked.

"Does it sound like it?"

James narrows his eyes and Danny tenses his shoulders.

"Yes."

He replies, trying not to sound as scared as he feels.

"Good."

Says James, nodding his head.

With that, he leaves the diner and Danny soon follows.

In Her Shadow

He doesn't think he will be going back there again.

In Her Shadow

Chapter 8: Pretty As A Postcard

"Mommy, can I have a cookie?"
It's the day of the picnic and Jenny, James and Dahlia have just found the 'perfect' place to lay their blanket.
Dahlia is all smiles and Jenny and James even more so because they get to spend time with her; as a couple.
"Don't you want a sandwich first, sweetheart?"
Jenny asks, pointing to the picnic basket.
"They have your favourite on them."
James says, taking one out for her.
"Peanut butter and strawberries?"
"Strawberry jam, yes."
She dances in excitement as he hands her the sandwich.
"Mmm.. do the ducks like them too?"
"No, sweetheart. We can feed them grapes later."
Jenny says, and James gives her a funny look.
"What?"
She asks.
"Grapes."
He says.
"You're going to feed grapes to the ducks?"
"Yes, sliced grapes."
Jenny replies, like it was common knowledge; that's what ducks eat.
"Posh ducks."
James laughs.
"Our mum used to give us half a loaf of bread to feed them and that was our day out."

Jenny smiles.

"My dad did the same thing but it turns out, bread is bad for them."

She says.

"And sliced grapes?"

He asks.

"Are healthy and easy to digest."

She says, rubbing her tummy.

James bites his lip in wonder.

"So."

He says, trying to let it sink in.

"Essentially, what you are saying is... the ducks are on a diet?"

Jenny thinks about this and then nods.

"Oh, how times have changed, love. I blame the media."

Jenny giggles as she pictures little ducks with fashion magazines and James wraps his arm around her and pulls her close.

They sit back and watch as Dahlia makes a mess with the peanut butter; this is something they could get used to, more happy times like this. They looked like they could model for a postcard that read, 'wish you were here' but they didn't wish anyone else was there. They were a lovely family as they were. Passers by told them so.

James almost forgets that Jenny is sick until he takes her hand and he sees that her skin is more pale than his. They used to joke about the possibility of him being a vampire because he wore all black, preferred night to day and his skin was as pale as the moon was; next to the silky, black sky. They thought it impossible to get a whiter shade than his skin but sitting beside her now; James gives Jenny the winning title of, 'the palest skin ever'.

"You okay, love?"

He whispers, so Dahlia won't hear.
"I'm fine."
She replies.
"It's just, you're-"
"I'm the happiest I'll ever be, James. Let me enjoy it."
He nods and tries not to think too much into her words. If he did; he would wonder if that meant she wouldn't be equally as happy on their wedding day, or if they would be married at all.

He can't think about it.

"Dahlia, love, would you like to hear a story?"

It's Jenny's turn to give a funny look and Dahlia takes a seat in between them to hear what he has to say.

"When I was your age – which was a very long time ago – my mum used to take me to a park, that was very much like this but a little smaller and-"

"What about your daddy?"

Jenny squeezes James' hand. They had never explained to Dahlia that, not everyone gets two, loving parents and James squeezes back; deciding not to make today the day, that she finds out.

"Well, my daddy worked far away so, he couldn't come with us but-"

"Why did he do that?"

It takes him a second to realize, she doesn't mean why did his dad walk out when James was a baby and that she meant, why did he work so far away.

"Well, there weren't that many jobs where I lived, love."

"Will you ever go far away?"

"Dahlia, let James finish his story, sweetheart."

He smiles at them both.

"Well, she – my mum – used to take me, my brother and two sisters to the park and we would all squeeze onto the bench that was closest to the pond; so we could feed the ducks.

One of the days we went there and we were sitting on that very bench, when a little duck came out of the water and it bit my mum on the toe-"

"The duck bit her toe?"

Dahlia's mouth hangs open in disbelief and Jenny tries to stifle a giggle.

"You can laugh, Jennifer but you know what my mum did?"

"What?"

They ask, in wonder.

"She took her sandal off, waved it at the duck and told it off."

He says, chuckling.

"I swear to God, she told this little duck he was a bad duck for biting her toe and do you know what the duck did then?"

They shake their heads.

"It bit her toe again."

He says, and they all roar with laughter and there are tears streaming down James' face as he is laughing too hard at the memory.

"You're making that up."

Jenny says, shoving him.

"No, Jennifer, honestly. I remember it so clear and I remember it now because, my mum didn't think it so silly to tell a duck off – while waving her sandal at it – and yet, I find it absurd that we are going to feed grapes to them later."

He gives her a little shove back.

"I think even my mum would have raised an eyebrow at that one, love. And she was quite mental."

He sits back, smiling.

"Well, maybe that's why the duck bit your mom's toe."

Jenny says.

"Maybe it was letting her know that, bread isn't good for them."

James laughs again.

"Well, that was one ungrateful duck, I tell ya!"

Dahlia tugs on James' shirt.

"James, is your mom my grandma?"

He looks to Jenny for the answer and she doesn't know what to say as she knows if he was to say no, she would ask why and so on but if he says yes, they will have to explain that she is no longer with them.

"Well..."

He starts.

"Yes!"

Jenny finishes for him.

"She is, sweetheart but she lives in the sky with the stars."

Dahlia sits for a moment, trying to think of what to ask next. She has nothing.

"We will visit her soon, mommy."

Jenny tries to hold back her tears. Tears that she doesn't ever want Dahlia to see.

"Hey, why don't we get those grapes and go find the ducks eh?"

James says, distracting Dahlia; as Jenny lets a few tears, escape from her eyes.

"I want to see if they'll actually eat them."

He starts to pack up the picnic so they can go to the duck pond and as he helps Jenny up, it feels like lifting a pillow. She really has lost a lot of weight, he thinks.

"Are you up for this, love?"

She nods her head and smiles.

"I have to be."

He bites back tears of his own and tries to swallow the lump in his throat as he watches Dahlia, skipping in front;

unaware of the sadness that follows behind her.

They didn't look like a postcard now. They looked like the lead up to the end of a sad movie and James didn't want those credits to roll anytime soon.

Hand in hand, he and Jenny walk in a silent, brooding bubble and not even the laughter of Dahlia – as she hopped, skipped and jumped along in glee – could penetrate it.

The end was creeping up on them.

They reach the duck pond and find the bench closest to it, just like James used to do with his mother.

Dahlia sits first. She thought the ducks would just wander over to her and grows confused when they don't.

"Why are they still in the water, mommy?"

She asks, tilting her head to the side.

James ruffles her hair.

"They have to see the food first, love."

He says.

"If you don't have some treats, they go looking for someone who does."

Jenny reaches into the picnic basket and brings out a box of grapes and James still can't quite believe the ducks will eat them.

"You actually did slice them, I thought you were joking."

She nods and hands them over to Dahlia, encouraging her to throw some in and notices that James is just as excited to feed the ducks as she is.

Her heart goes out to him. It couldn't have been easy for him, growing up without a father and his mother dying when he was in his teens. Such tragedy and yet, from it; came this brilliant man who was full of love and never short on smiles.

She turns her thoughts to her own situation and wonders how Dahlia will turn out – if she would be able to cope – when she is gone. William doesn't have a new girlfriend –

someone who could be a stepmother to Dahlia – and her own family don't speak to her. They cut all ties with her when she married William because she did so, against their wishes. They thought he was 'much too old for her and preying on her vulnerability'.

Her eyes sting as more tears start to form but this time, she doesn't let them fall.

She keeps on smiling as she watches joy spread across the faces of her most favourite people in the world and she takes comfort in knowing that; no matter what, her little girl will still have someone to love her, when she is no longer around.

"You not going to throw some in, love?"

James asks, pulling her down from her cloud of thoughts.

"They're really lapping them up, who would have thought?"

He offers the box to her and she takes one slice from it and throws it to the duck who is the furthest away.

This melts James' heart.

"You never let anyone go without, do you, love?"

She shakes her head and he hands the box back to Dahlia, as he sits back with Jenny. He tries not to think about her pale skin or the way her eyes are watering now but rather; he thinks about all the things he loves about her and all the good memories they have created together.

Soon her body will leave him and he won't wake up to the feel of her skin against his but, he won't let her die. Her heart and her soul; he will carry them with him for the rest of his life. A life – he thinks – will not be worth anything, if Jenny is not there to share it with him.

He sinks so deep into his thoughts that he doesn't realize, tears have started to spill from his own eyes. He only notices when he feels Jenny's cold hand, gently wipe them away. Her hands have become like that of a porcelain doll, he thinks. So pale and so cold but they are still just as soft as the first time;

she ever touched her hand to his skin.

He smiles.

"I'm sorry, love."

She continues stroking his face.

"I know."

She shivers and not before time. They are sitting in a park in November and so, shivering is to be expected. James believes it's more than the cold though. He thinks it's just a reminder that she's slowly fading away. He whips his jacket off and wraps it around her and normally she protests; not wanting him to be cold too but today, she really needs the extra warmth.

It's time to head home.

James parks outside their house and before he can get out of the car himself; William is there, taking Dahlia out of the back seat.

He jumps out and goes around to the passenger side to get the door for Jenny and when William sees her, he can't look her in the eye.

"We're only just back, mate."

James says, standing in front of Dahlia.

"We were going to have dinner together and-"
"Well, I decided it's time she was home with me."

James bites his lip.

"Jennifer, love, can you take Dahlia inside so I can have a little chat with her daddy?"

Jenny nods, not really having the strength to have a chat with him herself and William watches as she slowly walks up the path.

"Why are you doing this?"

James hisses.

"What?"

William asks.

In Her Shadow

"Why am I picking my daughter up to take her to her home?"

"You said she could come here today, you said -"

"I did and she did and now it's time for her to come home."

James takes a deep breath and steps away. He doesn't want to get so angry again that he can't control himself. He doesn't want to hit him again.

"You know, you keep saying that."

He says, shaking his head.

"You keep saying 'home' as if she doesn't have a home here too. She will always have a home here."

William purses his lips.

"And when Jen is dead?"

James feels like he has just jumped into a freezing cold lake, with no clothes on. He can't believe someone could be so callous and say such a statement, without any emotion behind it.

"How can you ju-"
"No, James, how can you expect me to leave her here?"

William whispers.

"Especially when you said yourself that Jen fears Dahlia could find her dead and beyond that; she won't always have a home here because like I said before, you're nothing."

James leans against his car, too weak to stand on his own. He thought they were making progress, mending bridges and that they would both think about what's best for Jenny, from then on.

He feels a sense of betrayal — as much as that thought annoyed him — he thought that everything was going to get better.

He realizes now just how gullible he could be. He really wasn't a bad guy; he was a softy at heart and believed in romance and long term friendships. He didn't want to have bad blood with anyone but William – he sees now – will never count him as or want him to be part of Dahlia's life and that, just isn't fair.

He hangs his head.

"Fine."

He sighs.

"But can you live with the guilt of depriving that little girl of spending time with her mum, while she still can?"

William nods sharply.

"Send her out."

James traipses through the house and when he gets to Jenny and Dahlia, all he can do is shake his head. He is devastated for Jenny, she doesn't deserve this.

Jenny takes Dahlia's hand.

"Sweetheart, why don't you find some cartoons to watch."

She says, sitting her down on the sofa.

"I'm just going to see your daddy for two minutes and tell him what you're having for dinner."

James looks to her, surprised at her sudden burst of energy and goes to follow her outside but she places a firm hand on his chest and stops him in his tracks.

"Not your battle, baby."

He opens his mouth to argue his case but she stops his words from flowing, with a soft kiss.

"It will be okay."

She marches on out and William is confused at the sight; wondering where his daughter is but before he could ask her anything, she grabs him by the throat and slams him against James' car.

"Listen."

She starts, her voice filled with power; leaving him no choice but to, close his mouth and hear what she has to say.

"I have had enough of being afraid of you."

She continues.

"Dahlia is my daughter. I carried her for 9 months. I. Am. Her. Home. Do you hear me?"

William sinks from her grip, as if he were standing in quicksand and his legs were made of lead and he comes to a crouch.

"I didn't mean to hurt you-"

He whispers.

"Sing a new song, William, I've heard this one already!"

She snaps, and James, who has been watching from the window – making sure no harm comes to Jenny – makes his way out and takes her in his arms. He couldn't be more proud of his green eyed warrior and although she showed such strength just seconds ago, she trembles against his body now. He supports her as she allows herself to sink into his arms and William doesn't move. He has nothing to say. He – for the first time – recognises just how badly he has treated her.

"Chicken nuggets, curly fries and lots of sauce, mate."

James says, smiling down at him.

"That's what Dahlia will be eating tonight. Her favourite. In her home."

He leads Jenny up the path. Not wasting any time on looking back and inside they find Dahlia, sitting content with her cartoons and they smile a smile that comes all the way from the inside and sails straight to the outside.

Another 'happiest I'll ever be' moment, Jenny thinks.

Chapter 9: The Talk

It's the next morning and James has just gotten home from dropping Dahlia off at William's.

William seen that, he didn't have the strength – or the right – to try and stop her from staying over last night. She was happy where she was and there was nothing he could have done about it.

Jenny and James have decided to take a day off from the diner and spend a full day; where it is just she and him. Something, they didn't get the chance to do often as she worked at the diner most days and as it was James who made her diner dream a reality; he dealt with everything else in between.

"Shall I make us a coffee, love?"

He joins her in the kitchen, where he sees that the kettle has already been boiled and he pulls a chair out from their breakfast table and motions for Jenny to sit. She does.

"It's awful cold out there today, by the way. Glad we won't be out in it."

Jenny watches as he fills her mug first. She liked that about him. That he was always so thoughtful to put her first but, she hated that about him too; she wished he would show the same care to himself, as he did to her.

"Did he give you any trouble?"

She asks., talking about William.

James snorts at this, as he passes her cup to her.

"Course not."

She smiles.

"So no more fighting?"

In Her Shadow

He takes the seat across from her and smiles back.

"I don't think so, love."

They both take a sip from their cups at the same time and try to figure out how to approach the conversation, they stayed home to have. James puts his cup down first.

"Love... I wouldn't mind, you know, if you wanted to wait."

He says, not wanting her to feel pressured into doing this. "There's plenty of time to-"

"There isn't though!"

She snaps, slamming her mug down.

She didn't mean to snap. She didn't even realize she was going to but she couldn't take it back.

They let those words hang in the air for a couple of minutes. Unable to find something to say, that would take away the urgency of them. Jenny takes another sip of her coffee but James has lost the taste for his; he pushes it to the side.

"So, we talk about it now."

He says, accepting that; this was something, they just had to do.

"Yes."

She replies.

"We talk about it now."

James stretches his arms across the table and places his hands, so that his palms are facing upwards. Jenny hesitates before she places her hands on top of them. Palm to palm, their hands never fit the way they did in the movies. Her hands were slightly bigger than his but he always had a way of making them feel smaller, more dainty and cosy inside his.

She feels ready.

"You can ask whatever you need to know."

She says, passing the buck to him.

James runs his thumbs over her knuckles and swallows

away a lump that formed in his throat, when he was practicing the question in his head.

"You haven't told me yet, what it is you-"

"Cancer. Lung."

She throws the words at him, as if she were ordering off of a menu in a busy restaurant. He squeezes her hands.

This was the last thing he expected. A disease he believed only plagued those who were smokers or much older. Jenny hadn't smoked a day in her life and she was only 26; he couldn't get his head around it.

"Did they tell you..."

He starts, unable to finish. He thought he wanted to know the answer but the fact that it was just seconds away, changed his mind. He'd rather not know.

Jenny picks up on this.

"I didn't want to know either so, I asked them not to tell me."

She says, shrugging her shoulders.

She tries to release one of her hands, to wipe the tears that were dripping from James' face but he won't let go. He can't let go.

Jenny didn't want this. She didn't want to make him cry and she didn't want him to see her cry. She almost wishes she didn't tell him in the first place but she couldn't do that to him. She wanted him to be prepared; she didn't want it to hurt him more than it had to. She didn't know if anyone could ever prepare for something like this though. The end.

"James..."

He looks up. The look in his eyes clutches at her heartstrings. She always told him he had Labrador eyes, that he was like that loyal dog that never left your side and was always happy to see you. This time, he looked like an abandoned puppy. Bewildered and no happy home to take shelter in. In leaving, she would be taking away his collar and making him a stray. When she put it like that in her mind, she lost a little love for herself.

He pandered to her every need, made sure she was always safe from harm and in return; he asked for nothing.

She changes the direction of the conversation.

"James, did I love you enough?"

He tilts his head to the side – not swaying her from further comparing him to a puppy – and tries to understand, where this question is coming from. He wondered why she thought she had to ask. Wondered if he made her feel like he wasn't loved enough because that was far from the case. After his mother died, he never thought he would find a love like the love she had for him. Eternal, warming and unconditional. But he did. He found that love with Jenny and now she was asking, if she loved him enough. He's perplexed.

"Jennifer, love... I don't know what to say."

He says, his voice uneven.

"Of course. More than enough."

She looks to their hands, still holding on.

"You weren't my shadow."

She sighs.

"You were in my shadow..."

She squeezes his hands.

"I never let you shine, did I?"

He doesn't like that she's now speaking in past tense. She is still here, she loves him, she let's him shine.

"Listen to me."

He pulls himself closer to the table and brings his voice to a soft, gentle tone.

"I never had a home after my mum..."

He stops himself from using the word 'died'. Jenny nods and lets him continue.

"My sisters were grown with their own lives and babies to feed and my brother and I were shipped from pillar to post."

He shivers as the memory, plays out in his head.

"We were too young to go out and make a living on our own but too old to be adopted by the newly-weds; who wanted little, cute babies - who hadn't yet known anything of the world so, they couldn't answer back and be like someone else's kid."

His voice cracks.

"As opposed to their own."

He looks away, trying to fight the fresh tears that were coming now as he thinks about how he will never have a child of his own. He forces the thought from his mind and continues to his point.

"I never had much of anything really but, then I met you and suddenly; I had everything."

He smiles.

"You've shown me a life, that no movie, no book or other person on this planet could show me and-"

"Stop."

She snatches her hands out of his. She doesn't want him to continue. It'll only make it harder on him and also, she doesn't want him to be so nice to her. Not anymore. She doesn't want to feel bad about leaving him; even though she wasn't given a choice. She wants to leave knowing that he's strong, that he can stand on his own two feet and most importantly; that he can carry on without her. She doesn't want to hear his stories of what his life was like before her. She's already heard them as he never stopped reminding her how much she meant to him and that his life only started meaning something, when she walked into it.

She wanted to hear that it'll still mean something when she is no longer here to share it with him. She wants him to know his worth too.

"Why do you never speak to yourself this way, James?"

She asks.

"Why do you paint yourself as the big, bad wolf and me; the little girl, in the red hood?"

He stands and takes his cup to the sink and starts washing it out.

"This isn't about me."

He says, trying to drown out the sound of his sniffling, with the running water.

Jenny gets up and stands behind him.

"It never is."

She sighs.

"It's always been about me and what you can do for me. You gave me your heart, you gave up wearing bright colours so you could truly be my shadow, you gave me the diner... let me give something back."

She ties her arms around his waist and rests her head against his back. He places the cup down and holds onto the counter to steady himself. He's still bamboozled about where this is coming from and even more so, where it is going. There's nothing she could give to him that she hasn't already and he needs her to understand that. She is everything.

"Jennifer... I have-"

"Shhh..."

She holds on to him tighter and gently sways. He sways along with her and to anyone on the outside looking in, they would look like they are moving to the rhythm of their favourite slow song but they are moving to the sound of silence; the saddest song of all.

They come to a stop as their tears dry up and facing each other now, Jenny leans in and steals a kiss.

She won't tell James what she is going to give him. Not

until she knows that she will be able to. She has a plan.

"I'm going to call my parents."

She says, as she escapes his embrace.

"They need to know."

James nods his head, unsure of what to say but he knows this is something she must do and all he can do is stand behind her, no matter what.

He had never met her parents. They were still under the impression that she was married to William so, he worried a little. He thought that they may not accept him and they will steal Jenny away; wanting her to spend her remaining days without him.

He says nothing and Jenny – knowing him well – knows exactly what he is mulling over in his mind. She smiles.

"They will like you."

She says, trying to put his mind at ease.

Truth is, she isn't sure if they will as; she didn't even know how they felt about her anymore, never mind a new fiancé.

"They will just need time to adjust."

James knew that time was running out and so wondered how her parents would even spend a thought on him, never mind time; getting to know him. He didn't know this was Jenny's plan.

He didn't know that her parents had been in touch through the years, wanting to get to know Dahlia but Jenny held a grudge against them. They disowned her. She didn't think she owed them anything but now, she was willing to grant them that access to their grandchild; if they did something for her in return.

First, she wants them to attend her wedding and second, she wants them to accept James. Keep in touch with him when she is gone and give him something he had been searching for, for so long; a family.

It would be her dying wish and the last thing she could give him that would mean so much to him.

He watches as she lets her thoughts consume her and he isn't as good at reading her, as she is him so he couldn't tell if her thoughts were happy or sad.

"Penny for them, love?"

He says, pulling her back into the room. She smiles and tucks her thoughts away for later.

"Sorry."

She says, giving herself a shake.

"Was in my own little world there."

He strokes her head and then her cheeks, secretly checking her temperature. She feels cold and clammy.

"Fancy a lie down?"

Jenny nods, suddenly feeling worn out.

He takes her hand and leads her to the bedroom. He fixes her pillows the way she likes them and pulls back the cover so she can get under and he could tuck her in. He eases himself in beside her, pulling her close and sharing his body heat. She holds on, not wanting to fall asleep yet as she was enjoying this moment but her head starts lolling as she loses the last of the strength she was clinging onto and she falls asleep in his arms.

James isn't tired. He's wide awake and just lies there; staring at the ceiling and every five minutes, he turns to watch Jenny's chest as it slowly rises and then falls again. Her breathing was getting more and more shallow by the minute and every second, he tried to prepare himself for that last breath and enjoyed the brief calm he felt; when it didn't come.

He wondered how many more times he would get to lie beside her like this. How many more times would she come in from the cold and slide her hands up his shirt to warm them, making him jump in the process. He cuddles in, trying to get closer than he's ever been and closes his eyes.

Sleep finally comes for him and with it, an unsettling dream.

He tosses and he turns and he cries for it to stop and this wakes Jenny. She takes his face in her hands and waits for him to feel her fingertips, gently tap against his cheeks. She always does this when he has a nightmare; so he can feel that outside the dream is what's real and he can wake up.

His eyes remain closed.

"James, sweetie."

She whispers in his ear.

"It's just a dream. Wake up."

His eyes snap open and the first thing he sees is Jenny's smile, as her face hovers just inches from his.

His heart – which had felt like it was about to burst – starts to beat at a regular speed as he realises that, he was only dreaming and he hadn't lost her yet. He caresses her neck, her shoulders and runs his hands down her arms until he is holding her hands.

"Sorry, love."

He whispers groggily.

She thinks about asking him what he dreamt of but decided it was best not to as, she could only imagine.

"It's okay. You're okay."

She soothes.

He squeezes her hands and looks up at her with sad eyes. He didn't want her to worry about him.

He looks to the clock on the bedside and sees they have been sleeping for around three hours and his sadness turns to contentment as he was granted the gift, of waking up beside her again.

"Did I wake you, love?"

He asks, hoping that he hadn't.

"No. I got up about ten minutes before I noticed you were having a nightmare."

She replies, not wanting him to worry about waking her. She was glad he did. She didn't want to miss out on time they could be spending together, for sleep. She would get plenty of that soon enough, she thinks. But, not now.

"Will you sit with me when I call my parents?"

He sits up, still holding her hands safely in his.

"Of course."

He nods.

"When you wanting to call?"

"Now."

She says, taking her hands back and making her way out of the bed.

He nods again.

"Okay, love. I'm right here."

He follows her as she makes her way to the living room and sitting on the sofa, Jenny takes a deep breath and dials her parents number.

James puts his arm around her and squeezes her shoulder.

"Hello?"

She starts to shake.

"Dad?"

Silence.

"Dad?"

James looks concerned.

"Dad, it's me."

She says.

"Please, don't hang up. It's important."

She sniffs back some tears.

"Daddy, I know you're there listening... Please."

She sighs.

"Talk to me."

She's about to give up when she hears a fragile voice on the other end."

"Dad?"

She squeezes James' knee as she listens to the voice.

"No, she's okay but-"

She squeezes harder."

"I know but, dad, I need to see you. I need you to meet someone and I need-"

She listens again.

"His name is James."

James bites his lip and doesn't know where to look.

"I need to see you, dad."

She says again.

"Mom too. I need to see you both and it has to be soon."

James strokes her hair as her voice becomes more desperate.

"Ask her, please..."

She waits for a response.

"What did she say?"

Her knees start to shake as she listens.

"You're sure?"

She hangs up the phone, not even saying goodbye and James concludes that's because; one wasn't said to her. Jenny isn't rude.

He stays silent, waiting for her to speak first.

"How would you feel..."

She turns to him.

"If I asked you to go with me to visit them."

She takes a deep breath.

"Tomorrow?"

She sighs.

James is delighted for her. Her parents want her to visit and he is so happy about that but he is nervous that it was so soon. He knew it had to be though.

"I would go anywhere you asked me to, love."

He smiles.

"Tomorrow, is it then?"

She nods and goes from sitting rigid to, lying down and resting her head in his lap.

"Tomorrow."

She says.

He strokes her hair as she drifts off to sleep once more and this time, he stays awake. He turns his thoughts to tomorrow and can't seem to derive any positivity from them so, he gives up trying and silently accepts that; this could all go belly up.

Chapter 10: Jenny's Parents

As James drives he and Jenny to her parents home, his tummy is in knots. On one hand, he is elated for her to be spending time with them and on the other; he is worried it won't be a pleasant experience for Jenny or that, they may not like him.

"We expecting much today, love?"

He asks.

"I mean, they'll be keen to see you, right?"

Jenny isn't sure. Her dad didn't sound excited over the phone but it's the first she has spoken to him in a few years so, that was to be expected.

"Baby steps."

She says, and James thinks about the last time she said this to him; on the day she accepted his proposal. His tummy knots even more as he can't stomach the thought of her maybe asking them to come to the wedding and them rejecting her invite. He doesn't know what he would do or say then.

"This is us, we are here."

She says, taking her seatbelt off.

James takes in the scenery as he steps from the car and as he opens the door to let Jenny out; he catches a glimpse of someone watching them from the window of the big, white house across the street. He thought it may have been a nosy neighbour until Jenny starts making her way towards that house.

He had parked on the wrong side and he contemplates

getting in the car and parking again but that would mean leaving Jenny to walk in alone. He leaves the car where it is and follows her.

The person watching; doesn't leave the window and James pretends not to notice as he gets closer and closer.

They stop at the door and Jenny knocks. While they wait for someone to answer, James thinks about what it would've been like if this was his mother. He knows she would most definitely be running out to greet them, hugging Jenny and whisking her inside to welcome her to the family. He feels strange that it isn't the case here and it bothers him that Jenny has to even knock and wait awhile, before anyone could be bothered to answer; especially when they knew they were standing there. It saddened him.

The door creeks open slowly and a woman steps out on to the path. She is smaller than Jenny but James could definitely see they resembled each other. This was her mother.

"How much?"

The woman asks, and James is thrown by her question as he picks up on the fact that, she thought Jenny was here for money. It also didn't sit well with him that, she wasn't invited inside; she wasn't welcomed.

Jenny doesn't get any of that yet.

"Mom."

She says, through gritted teeth.

"Where's dad?"

The woman thrusts an envelope at her.

"This enough?"

The penny finally drops and Jenny throws the envelope back.

"I've never asked you for anything."

She snaps.

"How could you even..."

James catches her as she stumbles back in disbelief but her mother doesn't even flinch.

"And him."

She says, pointing to James.

"Why can't he go out and make you money?"

James drops his jaw.

"You've got this back to front."

He says, offended.

"Jennifer isn't here for your money. I am not here for your money, we-"

"I'm dying, mom..."

Jenny cuts in and this time, her mother flinches. She looks like she has just been thrown a ball that was too heavy to catch so, she dodges it and lets it land at her feet.

The person who was watching them from the window, now pushes his way out of the door and takes the woman by the elbow.

"Let them in, June."

He says, and leads them all inside.

Their home is bigger than any home James has ever seen and he couldn't imagine Jenny living somewhere like this. She didn't like fancy things and liked to keep things cosy. All this space felt cold to him; like a showroom and he laces his fingers with Jenny's, so they won't be separated. This place made him uneasy.

"You okay, love?"

He whispers, before they enter the living room.

She pulls him inside and they sit, awkward and not really sure what to say so they wait for her parents to speak first.

Her dad shakes his head and takes his glasses off.

"What happened to William?"

They all look at him in shock. Not quite believing that's the first thing he asked, after Jenny revealed she is dying.

"Told you, he wasn't good."
He continues.
"And is this?"
He nods to James.
"A new one?"
He asks.
Jenny squeezes James' hand and fights her tears. She doesn't want them to see her cry, she wants to be strong.
James squeezes back.
"This is James."
She says calmly.
"We have been together for two and a half years and-"
"The boy not got a tongue?"
Her dad interrupts.
James clears his throat and sits forward slightly.
"Sir, we came here today because - because..."
He didn't know what to tell him. This was Jenny's moment and he didn't want to steal it from her but also, he didn't want her to feel like she was fighting this battle alone.
"Jennifer means more than the world to me, understand."
He says, finding his voice.
"And we have come here together."
He continues.
"She - to tell you what's been happening and I, to support her."
He takes a deep breath.
"We come here with the hope that maybe..."
He looks to Jenny.
"You'd be a part of her life again."
"What I have left of it."
She adds.
Her fathers face crumples and her mother lets out a soft sob. They're defences have been smashed and they see the

urgency of the situation.

James and Jenny manage to hold it together.

"Dad... Mom."

Jenny sighs.

"I never wanted this."

She says, genuinely.

"I didn't want Dahlia to miss out but-"

"Then why did you keep her from us?!"

Her mother cries.

Jenny clenches her jaw and James rubs her back.

"It wasn't as simple as that."

She replies.

"You know that, mom."

James doesn't pick up on the underlying accusation, she made to her mother in this statement and he clears his throat to take over.

"Dahlia doesn't live with us."

He says, and Jenny's father is dazzled by his statement.

"What do you mean?"

He asks, putting his glasses back on; as if this would make him see the situation, more clearly.

Jenny wipes her face.

"He keeps her from me too."

Silence.

Jenny's dad stands and walks over to them both. He places his hand on Jenny's shoulder and gives James a look that requests him to move so he can sit beside her. James hesitates but he does as the man wants and watches as he cradles her and she sinks into his arms. Baby steps.

Jenny's mother doesn't move. She watches too and James hovers in the centre of the room.

"Dad, you knew."

Jenny whispers.

"You warned me but I-"
He stops her.
"Your heart couldn't be swayed."
He says.
"Often, our hearts betray us."
He throws a glance at Jenny's mother and James detects a hidden meaning behind his words; like he wasn't just applying them to Jenny's situation but to his own also. Jenny was a daddy's girl. Her mother was the hard faced one, James definitely got that.
"And this one?"
He asks
"James?"
James looks to his feet.
"My heart was right with this one, dad."
Jenny smiles.
"I'm going to marry him."
Her mother jumps to her feet and exits the room and James can't decide whether to put his hands in his pockets or leave them at his side so he stands, in an even more nervous state than before and alternates between both.
Jenny pulls away from her dad, who can't find anything to say. He doesn't know whether to congratulate them both, go after his wife or just sit and hold on to his daughter; for as long as he can.
"This is the real deal, dad."
James comes to a crouch before them.
"I swear if things were different."
He says, looking her dad in the eye.
"I would have came to you and asked your permission first, sir."
Her dad believes this. There was something about James that he liked and he isn't usually easy to please so he must be

In Her Shadow

special, he thinks.

"Then, you'll have to ask me now."

He responds.

James throws Jenny a frightened look. This is it, he thinks. This is where her father would decide he didn't like him and maybe Jenny would have second thoughts about him too as it was clear to see, she loved her father dearly.

"Sir-"

He whispers.

"Richard."

Her dad interrupts.

"Carry on."

James nods.

"Richard..."

He starts, and feels weird that he is already calling him by his first name. He thought that had to be a good thing, surely.

"Your daughter... she's, she's exquisite."

He smiles at Jenny.

"I've never met anyone like her and I know I never will again and that's why I want -"

He shakes his head.

"No. I need to marry her. I need it."

He says.

"She's it for me."

Her father elbows her lightly.

"He's no Shakespeare is he?"

He says, causing Jenny to laugh. She needed this. She had missed his famous one liners badly and she was filled with so much happiness in that moment.

James nervously wrings his hands and Richard's eyes twinkle as he feels the love between them both. He smiles wide.

"You have my blessing."

He nods, and James drops to his knees – abandoning all sense of pride – and lays his head on Jenny's lap. She strokes his hair and Richard gets up to go find his wife.

"I knew my dad would like you."

James looks up.

"And your mum?"

She shrugs.

"I don't really care."

He accepts this. He could see she didn't as she has her father on her side and he knew that was all she needed. Her mother would never be like James' mother and he hates that he keeps comparing them but, it wasn't fair that Jenny had to go through this. Little girls should have their mothers, he believed.

He turns his thoughts to Dahlia – who is much younger than he was, when he lost his mother – and his heart breaks a little. He couldn't imagine the hurricane that was about to hurtle through that little girl's world and take with it - the most precious thing she will ever know - her mother. He knew he himself wouldn't be able to brave that one and so, how was a child expected to? He just couldn't imagine.

"My mum would've adored you, love."

He whispers.

Later, they are driving home and the atmosphere in the car is much more relaxed.

Jenny didn't get to see her mother again. She refused to come back and her dad profusely apologised for this. It wasn't his fault.

They were both in high spirits as not only did they have his blessing to marry; he had accepted Jenny's invitation to attend and walk her down the aisle.

She hugged him tight before she left and he shook James' hand; a gesture that meant the world to he and Jenny.

"Are you happy, love?"
James wondered.
"Overwhelmingly so."
She replies.
"Me too."
He smiles.

They drive on in silence. They're all talked out for the day and Jenny stares out of the window, hoping to catch a glimpse of the moon as it rises.

When she was little, she believed that there was a man who stood with a hose and changed day to night with it. Like they just poured out like water and it was as simple as that. She leans her head against the window and smiles. She would like to still believe in that, that things were that simple so she doesn't want to see the moon rise. Instead, she will keep searching for the little man with the hose and be amazed when the night sky, replaces the day sky.

It could be that simple, if she wanted it to be.

In Her Shadow

Chapter 11: The Angel In The Locket

"Milk, no sugar please."
It had been awhile since Danny had seen Jenny as he told himself he wouldn't go back to the diner but today, he really wanted to see her. He missed her.
"To stay or go?"
She asks, not as enthusiastic to see his face, as he was hers.
He is disappointed that she doesn't know this by now, that she doesn't ask him how he is doing or anything like that but, he doesn't let it show.
"To stay."
He sighs.
"I'll bring it over."
He takes his usual seat and James appears from the kitchen and for once, is surprised to see him there.
"Milk, no sugar, love? I'll take it to him."
Jenny hands him the cup and he takes it over to the table.
"Why don't you make like your day job and be history, eh?"
Danny smirks.
"You thought you would frighten me, didn't you?"
James lowers his voice.
"Your next coffee is in a 'to go' cup, got it?"
"And if it's not?"
Danny provokes.
James places his hand on the table and leans close to him.
"Then it'll be through a tube, in the hospital."
He walks away, leaving Danny to ponder if he is being serious. He figures that he is and doesn't know what to do

about it. He thinks he should tell Jenny but then, that might make him look scared or maybe – he thinks – she won't want to be with such a thug like James and take pity on him.

"Everything okay?"

Jenny breaks into his thoughts and he turns his attention to her. She's standing beside him with a smile on her face. The same smile, she uses for all of her customers.

"Yeah, everything is fine."

He nods.

"Listen, can we talk?"

This request takes Jenny by surprise as she couldn't guess what he wanted to talk to her about. She didn't even know him.

"About?"

He scoots close to her.

"James.

He says, from the side of his mouth.

"He hasn't been very nice to me and-"

"Let me get you a 'to go' cup for that and you can tell me all about it, on your way out."

She says, not letting him finish.

He's startled at her snippy tone and before he gets a chance to protest, she is pouring his coffee into the other cup.

"You creep me out, you know?"

She doesn't hold back.

"I don't want you coming in here again."

He looks offended.

"I creep you out?"

She nods.

"Yes."

She says.

"You sit there and you eye me up as if I come on the menu too. Well, I don't."

He springs to his feet and is about to answer her back when James steps in front of her.

"What?"

He asks, staring him down.

Danny has nothing. He doesn't want to argue with James because it's like he determined all along, he was shifty and who knows what the guy could do to him. He leaves with his tail between his legs and this time, he definitely wouldn't be returning.

James laughs.

"I only said, 'what?'"

"Yes, and the rest."

Jenny replies, letting him know that she heard his previous threat and he feels bad.

"I wouldn't actually-"

"You would."

She nods.

"I'm not complaining though. You're just looking out for me."

She makes her way back behind the counter and starts serving her customers. James can't take his eyes off of her as she smiles at every one of them and makes sure they're having the best dining experience. She truly is a warrior and he still can't quite believe that someone like her, loves someone like him. This is something he will never figure out as he will never have the courage to actually ask her.

He starts cleaning the tables.

"James! James!"

He whips round and sees Dahlia smiling up at him. He didn't notice her come in and he wonders why she ran to him and not her mother first.

"Dahlia!"

He smiles.

"What's up, love?"

He scoops her off her feet and squeezes her tight.

"Daddy said you have something to tell me."

She says, her eyes dancing.

"And he said it was a big secret so I haven't told mommy."

James frowns.

"Where is your daddy, Dahlia?"

He asks, and before she can answer he feels a tap on his shoulder. He looks round to see William.

James puts Dahlia down.

"Dahlia, go see your mummy so I can talk to your daddy about the secret, okay?"

She hugs his legs and runs over to the counter. Jenny pretends she doesn't know her and asks her for her order. Dahlia plays along and they giggle as James and William make sure they are out of earshot.

"What's the game, Will?"

William shrugs.

"No game."

He says.

"Then what's the secret I'm supposed to tell her, eh?"

They lock eyes.

"Do you think I would do that?"

William whispers.

"Think I'd leave it to you to tell my daughter the bad news?"

James shrugs.

"I dunno."

He says.

"You're a pretty callous piece of-"

"I brought her so you can tell her about the wedding."

James steps back and observes him for a moment.

"That's it?"

He asks, not quite buying it.

"That's all you brought her here for?"

"Well, I didn't come here for that mud in a cup you call coffee."

Jenny overhears this and is hurt.

"You don't get to criticise anything!"

She snaps.

"Jennifer, love, it's okay. You know it's not true."

James tucks her hair behind her ear.

"But-"

"Dahlia is here to hear our news, love."

He takes both of their hands; reminding Jenny not to lose her cool, while her little girl is watching and he smiles.

"Tell you what."

He hands their hands to each other and steps back.

"I'll take over at the counter, get her daddy a coffee and you both can sit down and have a little chat."

He takes his voice to a whisper.

"You do it, love. This is a mummy and daughter moment to enjoy."

She nods slowly. Taking in his meaning and she realises that, she desperately needs this moment. There's not going to be many more like it.

"Okay."

She agrees.

"Right then."

He forces a smile.

"Will, come tell me how you like your 'mud in a cup'."

William reluctantly follows behind him as Jenny takes a seat with Dahlia.

"So, you're here to hear the news, sweetheart?"

Dahlia leans in.

"No. Daddy said there's a secret but not to tell you about

it."

Jenny grows suspicious. She can't think why he would say that to her and not have her go straight to Jenny, if it was about the wedding. She suspects he's up to no good.

"Well, your daddy has it wrong, sweetheart."

She says, ruffling her hair.

"James doesn't have a secret that I don't know but, we do have some good news to share with you."

Dahlia claps her hands.

"I'm going to be a big sister?"

She shouts so loud that James and William hear this too and James' heart shatters. He scoops some vanilla ice cream into a little bowl and excuses himself as he takes it over to their table.

"Um, I thought she might like-"

"No, sweetheart... that's not it."

Jenny says, trying not to break.

James admires how calm and collected she is, in this moment. He doesn't know what to say himself. He wishes that were the truth.

"It's vanilla."

He says, placing the bowl before Dahlia.

Jenny doesn't look at him. If she did that, she would crumble quicker than a kicked sandcastle. She turns to Dahlia.

"We – James and I – we are going to get married, sweetheart."

Dahlia shovels a big scoop of ice cream into her mouth and grabs her head.

This makes James and Jenny laugh, providing much needed light to the situation.

"Brain freeze, love?"

She nods her head.

"What are you like?"

says James.
She feels better and is now grinning from ear to ear.
"Can I be a princess?"
She asks, excitedly.
"Princess, love?"
"You and mommy will be the king and queen and you will need a princess."
Jenny smiles.
"Yes, you can be our princess."
She says.
"And daddy can be the prince?"
James and Jenny exchange a look. They hadn't discussed it but they knew that neither of them would want to invite him and they didn't know what to tell Dahlia.
"I think I would be more of a frog, right?"
William intrudes on their moment.
"You have customers."
He says, and James sighs.
"No rest for the wicked eh, Dahlia?"
He gives her a little tickle and smiles at Jenny before getting back behind the counter.
"Why don't you help him, sweetheart?"
Jenny says, wanting to be left alone with William.
"You like helping him remember the orders."
Dahlia doesn't need to be offered twice. She loved coming here and pretending she worked behind the counter with James.
Jenny nods for William to sit.
"What's this about, William?"
He raises his eyebrow.
"What do you mean?"
He shrugs his shoulders.
"Talking about some secret I've not to know about?"

He huffs.

"I'm trying to do something nice and I'm getting bombarded with questions."

"I asked you one."

He looks to James.

"One that he has already asked me."

Jenny purses her lips.

"I know you know."

She says, referring to her illness.

"Know what?"

He asks, pretending he hasn't a clue what she is talking about.

"Don't."

William nods.

"Okay, so I know."

He admits.

"What? You think I brought her here so she can know too?"

Jenny shakes her head.

"No. I think you want to make this harder than it needs to be."

She has grown tired of going around in circles with him but she always finds herself, hopping on that carousel and going along with it. She doesn't like him having the last word.

"You want to play your little games, get inside our heads... it's not going to work this time."

William smiles.

"I don't remember you being such a cynic, Jen."

She leans close to him.

"I'm surprised you remember anything, with the amount of times you crashed your head against mine."

His jaw clenches. He couldn't believe she was really bringing this up now and he didn't think it fair.

"That was the alcohol."

He starts to crack his knuckles, nervously.

"And the times you wrapped your fingers around my throat and squeezed; if I got home, five minutes late from work?"

She asks, not letting him away with that recycled excuse.

"You were sober then."

He runs his fingers through his hair.

"Not now. Don't do this now."

He pleads.

He doesn't feel remorse, not in the slightest. He just wants her to stop because he can feel the anger; starting to burn within him and he doesn't want to lose his head here. Not in front of his daughter.

He thinks this is Jenny's plan. He thinks maybe she wants Dahlia to see that side of him, so she won't love him anymore and cry for James.

Jenny isn't like that though. She fought for two years of Dahlia's life, to shield her from that side. She would never do that.

"I know I've wronged you."

William says, through gritted teeth.

"But I'm trying here."

Jenny chuckles.

"By granting me a visit from my daughter?"

She runs her hands over her stomach.

"A daughter I carried in my tummy for 9 months and always sheltered her from the big, bad storm that was hurricane daddy."

He grips the edges of the table.

"I would never hurt her!"

He spits.

"No, just her mommy."

She replies, not backing down.

"Rendering me too tired to play with her. Unable to feed her myself because I could barely lift my arms. You may not have hurt her, in the way you hurt me but you stopped her from having the mother she deserved."

William leans across the table.

"If I was that bad, Jen..."

He whispers.

"If it was that bad, why didn't you leave? Huh? Why didn't you pack up your bags in the middle of the night, take her from her bed and run to somewhere safe?"

Jenny looks to the ceiling as she collects herself.

"You know how many times I tried that?"

She looks back, staring him straight in the eye.

"It was half the number of the bruises I received when you caught me."

James has been keeping an eye on their conversation and he senses it's getting to dangerous territory and as he has Dahlia with him, he tries to devise a plan to get over there; without involving her. She doesn't need or deserve to see this.

"Hey, Dahlia."

He says, thinking fast.

"You know that table down the front?"

He points to an empty table ahead and Dahlia nods.

"Well..."

He smiles warmly.

"I heard that; if you sit at it long enough, watching the people who pass the window – and don't pay attention to anyone who is in here – you get something special from a magical being."

She looks at him, sceptical to his claim.

"What kind of magical being?"

She asks.

"Oh, a fairy, I think."

He says, trying to conjure up an image of a fairy.

"A magical fairy with bells and um... um... she will bring you something nice."

As she had a love for fairies and all things magical, she decides to believe him.

"So I just sit and look out the window and she will come?"
She asks.

"I'm sure of it, love."

She skips over to the table, the magic will occur at and James; marches towards the one Jenny sits at with William.

"Everything okay?"

He looks at William as he says this.

"Everything's fine."

Jenny answers.

He looks to her now and notices she has been close to tears and his blood boils.

"Can't help yourself, can you. You always have to-"
"James!"

Jenny cuts him off and reels him in. She doesn't want them to fight, she just wants things to be calm and peaceful for once.

William says nothing.

"What's Dahlia doing?"

Jenny asks, taking the focus away from the previous situation.

James tears his eyes away from William and focuses on Jenny.

"I told her if she sits there, a fairy will come and give her a treat."

Jenny laughs.

"Did you bring your tutu with you?"
She says.

"I knew I forgot something."

He replies.

They laugh together and William envies what they have. He still loved Jenny, in his own twisted way and he despised James; for loving her better.

"Do us a favour, will you, love?"

James says, nudging Jenny.

"Distract the kid, while I go and get something from the back, eh?"

She nods in response and gets up and goes to sit beside Dahlia.

James returns and sneaks up behind their table and places a gold necklace on it. He jingles the coins in his pockets, trying to make a sound that would sound like a fairy tinkering and taps Dahlia on the shoulder.

"Did you see her?"

He gasps.

Dahlia jumps up and looks around.

"No, where did she go?"

She cries.

"She only flew down for a second, love but she dropped this."

He picks the necklace up and hands it to her and he is filled with joy, when her little eyes light up.

"She left it for me?"

James nods.

"She did, indeed."

He says, smiling.

"A beautiful trinket for a beautiful girl. Shall I put it on you?"

She hands it back to him and lifts her hair as he clips it on, with shaky hands.

"You like it, love?"

He asks.

In Her Shadow

"It opens."

Realising it's a locket, Jenny helps her open it and there's a picture on either side. One shows Jenny, James and Dahlia and the other shows a lady; who Dahlia doesn't recognise.

"Who's the pretty lady, James?"

Dahlia asks, making him beam at her choice of words.

"I think that must be the fairy who left it for you, love."

He says, not ready to tell her who it really is.

Jenny takes a closer look and sees that it's his mother.

"I don't think that was a fairy, James."

She says, smiling softly.

"I think it was an angel."

William lets them have their moment before he sheepishly wanders over and tells them, it's time for he and Dahlia to leave.

"Okay."

Says Jenny, her tone dry.

"But, she will be staying with us tomorrow. We have wedding stuff to talk about."

Dahlia gets excited.

"Can I, daddy? Is it okay?"

She asks William.

"Of course, love."

James says, answering for him.

"Your mum and I want you here so it's okay with your daddy."

William shoots James a look before he takes Dahlia's hand and leads her out of the diner. He doesn't like that he is now powerless. He's not used to it.

It's the end of the night and Jenny and James have just got home.

They head straight upstairs; too tired to sit and watch TV in the living room and when they are under the covers, Jenny sighs.

"You okay, love?"

James asks.

"I'm just tired, is all."

She replies.

He understands. He was really tired himself so he could imagine, it would be ten times worse for her.

"That was a really nice thing you did tonight."

Jenny smiles.

"What's that?"

James asks, his mind scrambled.

"The locket."

She says.

"It was lovely and Dahlia was over the moon."

He takes her hand.

"It was my mother's."

He smiles.

"She always had a picture of my dad in the other side but I took that out."

Jenny looks at him confused.

"James, that's something you should have held onto. It's too-"

"If my mum were here, love, she would have insisted it went to Dahlia."

He smiles again.

"She would've doted on that little girl."

Jenny squeezes his hand. She knows how much his mother meant to him and that he didn't have much to remember her by. He manages to amaze her more each and every day.

"She will look after it."

She assures.

"She's not like other kids, it's treasure to her."

James nods.

"I know, love. Did you see her face? It was the most precious thing."

They both lie in silence as they recollect that moment. Indeed, it was precious. They kiss each other goodnight and as they drift off to sleep, they are happy.

Their dreams are pleasant and their bodies comfortable. They are most content.

Chapter 12: Playing Nice

"Wake up, love."

James kisses Jenny on the forehead and she opens her eyes to see him smiling the most beautiful smile, she has ever seen him smile.

There was something different about him but she couldn't tell what yet.

"What time is it?"

She asks, looking to the clock on the bedside; which reveals she has slept in.

"James!"

She hits him with her pillow as he laughs.

"I'm sorry, love."

He says, clinging onto the pillow.

"But it's absolutely necessary that we take the day."

She furrows her brow, waiting for him to explain himself and he traces his fingertips across her forehead; as if to smooth out the crease.

"It's here."

He says, taking her face in his hands and stroking the corners of her eyes with his thumbs.

"That you want the creases, love. Not on your forehead."

She rolls her eyes.

"I'd rather not have creases at all, thank you very much!"

He pretends to be offended.

"No laugh lines?"

He throws his hands up, dramatically.

"Aw, thanks very much, love. You said you loved mine, now

I feel old."

She smiles.

"I do love yours."

She says, reaching out to touch his face.

"The lines on your face are my most favourite lines to read."

James blushes as she kisses his cheeks.

"I'll miss this, Jennifer..."

He sighs.

Jenny drops her head as a serious atmosphere enters the room. She tried not to think about the things she would miss; she wasn't ready to miss them yet. She is still here.

"So, why are we taking the day?"

She asks, changing the subject.

James manages a slight smile.

"I thought it would be nice if we were the ones to pick Dahlia up from school and bring her here."

She likes this idea.

"I like it when you think."

He laughs.

"Thanks, I guess."

She rolls her eyes again and he copies her, causing them both to smile again.

"And what are we supposed to do until we pick her up?"

James grins.

"Well, my beautiful bride to be... we can discuss our plans for the big day."

He says.

"Christmas?"

She asks jokingly. Not realising that she's just given James something else to worry about; would she even be around to see Christmas day? He doesn't let Jenny into his thoughts.

"Ha Ha."

He says.
"You know what day I'm meaning."
"Obviously."
She laughs.

He studies her face, which doesn't seem to be giving anything away and he wonders if she really wants to marry him or if she is just going along with it to keep him happy; as she knows, she might not be around for that much longer anyway.

This last thought troubles him. He didn't mean to think of it that way and knows Jenny wouldn't be thinking that way at all. If she says she is going to do something, she will do it. She doesn't have it in her to lie.

"Cornflakes?"

Jenny frees him from his thoughts and stares blankly at him, waiting for him to reply. She knew he was deep in thought and lately; when he was thinking deep, it was never good so, she didn't ask what was going on in his head.

"What about them, love?"
he asks.
"Would you like some?"

He smiles. Jenny wasn't the best cook in the world so when she offered to do the breakfast, it was either cereal or toast – which she often burnt – and James loved this. He liked that he could cook and that she enjoyed his cooking as it meant, it was just one more way for him to look after her.

"I'll get it, love."
He replies.
"You want an omelette or something?"
"No, I'm not really hungry."
He drops his smile.
"Are you feeling okay?"
"Yeah. I just don't feel like eating."

In Her Shadow

"But-"
She touches her fingertips to his lips.
"Not hungry."
He sighs and gently wraps his fingers around her wrist.
"Me either."
He says.
"I'll just have these."
He playfully bites her fingers and she snatches her hand away, pretending to be frightened and although James picks up on her pretending; he doesn't like that look on her. It only reminds him of a time that she wasn't pretending. He stands up and walks to the door.
"I'm just going to call Will, love and tell him our plan, yeah?"
Jenny walks to him and hands him his mobile phone.
"Text him instead."
She says.
He takes it from her and shakes his head.
"I do that and he will say he never got it. Best to call, love."
She shrugs.
"Suit yourself, babe."
She sighs.
"Just thought you'd want to avoid actually having to speak to him. You know what he's like."
He nods.
"I know. It'll be fine."
He makes his way to the living room and calls the number.
"Will?"
He says down the phone.
"It's James. Listen..."
He rolls his eyes.
"I know but, listen. We want to collect Dahlia today and bring her here."

He waits for William to protest but is surprised to hear him say they could.

"What's that? When? Okay, I'll see you in about twenty minutes then. Right, cheers."

He disconnects the call and turns to find Jenny, watching him from the doorway.

"What's happening in twenty minutes?"

She asks, concerned.

"Oh, nothing to worry about, love."

He smiles.

"You see, kids aren't allowed to wear jewellery in school and Dahlia's had to leave her necklace at home so he asked if I could pick it up, 'cause she didn't want to take it off today."

Jenny purses her lips. If this was anyone else making such a gesture, she would be fine. She thinks William has a hidden agenda and isn't happy that James was so quick to comply.

She studies him for a moment.

"And that's all you're wanting out of this arrangement?"

She asks, expecting there to be more to it, on his end too.

James tilts his head to the side, giving her that 'sad puppy' look.

"I don't follow, love."

He says.

"Well, you're just going to collect the necklace and nothing else?"

He holds his head up straight again.

"What else would there be?"

"You tell me."

He really doesn't know what she is trying to insinuate.

"Love, if you want me to-"

"No. Collect the necklace, by all means."

She says, frustrated. She thought she made it clear that she didn't want anymore fighting and she thinks; that's exactly what's going to take place. A fight.

"But you can't expect me to believe that's all there is to it."

James doesn't know how to react. He hasn't done anything wrong and that's all there really was to it.

"You could come with me, if you like?"

She slams her fist against the door.

"I don't want to see him."

She snaps.

"Are you dense?!"

She bursts into tears and he takes her in his arms and lets her cry it out. He realises this isn't about him. He remembers reading that mood swings could be expected, with her condition.

He doesn't take offence to her tone and isn't angry with her. He understands – as best he possibly can – and kisses her head in reassurance.

He gets it.

"I'm so sorry. I – I –"

He strokes her hair.

"It's okay, love. It's not you."

This statement sends a wave of hurt to his heart. The woman he fell in love with is slowly fading away and the cancer is eating all of the goodness from her soul. He wasn't just going to lose her on the day that it consumed her completely – he was already losing her with every short breath, she took in preparation for it.

He buries his head in her shoulder, trying to stop the tears from falling down his face and the harder he tries to stop them; more and more push their way through.

They sob together.

After they are all cried out, they let each other go and get back to what they were previously doing. As if the sobbing didn't occur.

"I better get off, love."

He sighs, not really wanting to leave her.

"Get this necklace and get it over with, eh?"

She nods.

"Are you-"

"I'm fine."

He kisses her goodbye and sets off on his way.

Pulling up outside William's house, James beeps his horn. William doesn't show.

He beeps again and there's still no sign of him. He decides to call and before he can get an answer there, William opens his front door and waves for James to go to him.

James rolls down his window.

"In a hurry, mate."

He calls to him.

"Kettle is already boiled."

William calls back.

James grunts. He wasn't up for playing nice today but he figures he can at least try to fake it. He switches his engine off and steps out of the car.

"Can't be bothered with this today, Will."

He huffs.

"Just toss me the necklace eh?"

William makes his way to him.

"I'm not asking you to give blood or sell your soul, Jim I'm-"

"James."

William laughs.

"Didn't like that?"

James shakes his head and William can't help but feel amused.

"You always shorten my name."

He says.

In Her Shadow

"You're the only one who calls me 'Will', ya know that?"

James shrugs.

"I do now."

He looks at his shoes, as if he has just been told off by his father or a teacher.

"Can I get the necklace now?"

He asks, wanting to get away from him.

"One coffee, please?"

William sighs.

"We need to talk."

James snaps his head up, wishing William would just be straight with him.

"I don't know the steps to this dance, Will – William."

He says.

"Just tell me what it is you're after and leave out the cajolery eh?"

William nods.

"I want to know..."

He digs his fingertips into his palms.

"How long she's got."

Silence.

Neither of them can look at each other as their minds start to race. William doesn't know if he wants to hear the answer and James doesn't want to discuss this with him, or anyone really.

He knew he had to at some point though. He and Jenny had a child together and James wouldn't want Jenny to have to discuss it with him herself. She doesn't need or deserve the added stress.

He leans against the car.

"I don't know..."

William doesn't believe this.

"Oh, come on! You can't-"

"I honestly don't know and neither does Jennifer so, don't ask her."

William leans against the car too.

"So, she can go at any minute?"

He asks.

"As we all can, mate."

James replies.

"Don't hold it against her."

William shrugs.

"Wasn't intending to."

He says.

They look down opposite ends of the street, not wanting to see the pain in each other's eyes.

"You wanting that coffee?"

James shakes his head.

"No. Came for the necklace, didn't I?"

William reaches into his pocket and takes out the locket.

"Who's the woman anyway?"

He asks, handing it to James.

"My mum."

James bites his lip.

"Just wanted the kid to have something to remember us by."

"Us?"

"Jennifer and I."

William tuts.

"You're not going anywhere, are you?"

He asks.

"I mean, you're not going to abandon her are you?"

This catches James off guard.

"Do I have a choice in the matter?"

William nods.

"I wouldn't do that to her... or to Jen. She really does-"

He braces himself.

"Love you."

William didn't want James in Dahlia's life. He made that clear anytime he got the chance to but, Dahlia did love him and William could never hurt her. He always wanted to be the best father he could be and keep her happy and taking her away from James, would make her unhappy. He was the one that didn't have a choice really.

James slips the necklace into his pocket.

"I've not been trying to play daddy, you know."

He says.

"I know – I've always known – my place."

"I know."

"Might've been a crappy husband to Jennifer but I know you're a great dad to that little girl."

William hangs his head.

"It was never her fault, what I did. It was-"

"I know."

James would never dream of blaming Jenny for the way he treated her. He can't see why William has to clarify that. He concludes that, maybe it was more for his own sake. Maybe if he finally said it out loud, he could see how dreadful he was and that would somehow cleanse him. James wasn't about to baptise him though. He would never like him and couldn't even find an ounce of forgiveness in himself, to give to William. He is done here.

"Anyway..."

He says, pushing himself off of the car.

"I better get back. I'll drop Dahlia off tomorrow."

William smiles in agreement and before James drives off, he takes one last look at him and ascertains once more that; no, he will never like this man.

He drives away.

Once home, he finds Jenny curled up on the sofa and still wearing her pyjamas.

"You okay, love?"

She half smiles.

"Just tired."

He fits himself beside her and starts to massage her legs.

"Not a bad day out there, I thought it would be colder."

She doesn't say anything.

"I got the necklace, Dahlia will be pleased."

Still nothing.

"Do you want me to let you get some sleep?"

He asks.

"You'll be needing your energy for later."

She pulls her legs away from him.

"You don't know how I'm feeling, James."

He folds his hands in his lap and chooses his words wisely.

"You can tell me, love."

He says.

"Help me understand. I'm here for you."

She pushes herself up.

"I don't want you to be the one."

She covers his hands with hers and stares, deep into his eyes.

"I don't want you to be the one who finds me."

He swallows hard and tries to respond but suddenly, it's like he has forgotten how to speak. He shakes his head and takes his hands out from under hers and places them on top.

"I couldn't do that to you, James. Please, don't-"

"What are you asking here, Jennifer?"

He has found his words.

Jenny brings her face closer to his and tries to project her soul through her eyes. She wants him to see that she is still inside there but, she has become a prisoner of her slow, dying body. He has to see that.

"You just can't be the one, okay?"

He sticks to the green of her eyes and realises that, although he said she can talk to him about anything – and at any time – he didn't want to hear this.

"Jennifer, I'm not going to leave your side."

He says, firmly.

"You can't ask that of me."

She narrows her eyes.

"Even if it were my dying wish?"

He is stunned. The Jenny he fell in love with would never request such a difficult task.

"Even if it were your dying wish."

He sighs.

"I'm sorry, love."

She shakes her head. She knew that he would never agree to what she hadn't quite asked him yet but there was no point now. It would only make her remaining days harder for them both and she needed these times to be special.

She gave up on the notion of having him let her go early and go somewhere, where she was not.

She kisses his cheek.

"It's all me, James."

She whispers.

"It's still me in here."

He pulls her in for a comforting embrace and tells himself off in his mind. He used to love how perceptive Jenny was, how she could tell what was on his mind – without him giving her any clues – but now; it was something that unsettled him.

He didn't want her to know every little thought because he was afraid of what he would think next. He couldn't control those thoughts that briefly visited his mind. The ones that reveal his worst fears and question whether Jenny; is still there beside him or if it was just a copy of her, for the time being. A still life painting, which loses more life the more you look at it, he thinks.

He bites his lip.

"Will you be wearing white, love?"

She looks up at him.

"For the wedding?"

She asks, letting him change the subject.

"Yes, for the wedding."

He says.

She shakes her head.

"I was thinking we could switch, if that's okay?"

A smile sneaks up on him.

"What, you be the groom and I, the blushing bride?"

She smiles too.

"I don't think you could handle the heels, baby."

James grins.

"You're probably right."

He says.

"I'd give it a bloody good go though."

This image tickles Jenny's ribs and she begins to laugh uncontrollably.

It warmed James' heart to hear her laugh. It was one of the things he loved most about her as it was contagious and always had him creasing up too.

"Aw, could you just imagine it, love?"

He says, in between laughs.

"My toes would be poking out all ways."

Tears start to stream down her face. Happy tears, brought on by the laughter.

"I'd love to see that."

She says, between gasps for air.

He takes her hand and watches her as she tries to regulate

her breathing again. Even now, she was beautiful to him and all thoughts he had previously – of her not being the same Jenny – vanish. She was every bit the Jenny he had fallen in love with and he would keep fighting alongside her; in her battle to cling onto life.

There was no doubt in his mind about that.

"So, switching?"

He asks, and Jenny collects herself.

"Yes."

She says.

"I was thinking, I could wear black for a change and you could shine in white... if it's okay?"

He smiles. If she wished it that way, he would do it.

"Love, I would wear a plastic bag if you asked me to."

She chuckles.

"Save that for another time."

She says, running her fingers through his hair.

"I just think it would be nice for you to take centre stage for awhile."

James snorts.

"Jennifer, you could wear that plastic bag and you'd still be centre stage."

She shoves him lightly.

"If that was all I was wearing, yes. Human nature and all of that."

He grins.

"Animal nature, love."

She leans in and kisses him. Softly at first and then full of passion, as if it were the last thing she would ever do.

James indulges in the kiss for a moment, before pulling away and tucking her hair behind her ears.

"What colour will Dahlia wear?"

He asks, jumping back into wedding talk.

Jenny folds her arms and huffs.
"I'm not made of glass, you know."
She scolds.
"You can still kiss me like - like that!"

James hangs his head and sighs. He didn't want her to feel undesired as he desired her very much but, he found it hard to engage with the kind of passion he used to. It makes him sad when he kisses her and runs his fingertips down her neck and arms; just to feel bone and a skin like marble.

He didn't know how to articulate this in a way that would make her understand that, it's not her. It's just hard for him.

"Love, I-"

"What? The taste of imminent death too bitter for your palate?"

He tenses his body and prepares for a barrage of harsh words thrown at him. Words he knows, she doesn't really mean but he will take them anyway. If it helped her, he would even assign himself the duty of being her personal punching bag.

Anything, to help her through.

He finds her silent.

She doesn't want him to answer. She wants to forget she said such a thing because that wasn't what she planned on saying. She only wanted him to know that it was okay to touch her.

"Will be time to collect Dahlia soon."

He says, shifting slightly.

"Will leave in about half an hour, if you want to come along?"

She shakes her head.

"I will stay here. I have to get dressed and tidy up a little."

He stands.

"Well, I can do that. What needs doing?"

In Her Shadow

She stands to face him.

"I want to do it."

He pulls her in for a hug and although he can feel her spine – protruding through the skin of her back – he runs his hands down it anyway.

His touch warms Jenny and they hold on tight, until he has to leave.

Chapter 13: It's Not My Birthday

James holds the car door open and helps Dahlia inside, fastening her seat-belt.

"Good day, love?"

She nods and settles in as he closes the door and gets behind the wheel.

"I told a story in front of everyone."

She says.

"Wow! In front of everyone?"

James asks.

"I could never do that, love. Well done!"

He praises.

"What was your story about?"

Dahlia is excited that he is taking an interest.

"Mommy the queen, James the king, Princess Dahlia and daddy frog."

He laughs out loud at this. He remembers when she asked to be a princess at the wedding, the last time she was at the diner.

"Don't think your daddy would be thrilled with that one, love."

He looks at her in the rear-view mirror and gives her a smile.

"Daddy said he's the frog."

She replies.

"He said that mommy just didn't want him to be a prince so he's a - a big, slimy frog."

James chews on the inside of his cheeks.

In Her Shadow

"Why didn't mommy want him to be a prince?"

She asks, tilting her head to the side.

He flashes her another smile in the mirror.

"Well, love, it's like this; your daddy preferred the role of the frog, you see? He didn't really want to be a prince and your mummy seen this."

"So she didn't kiss him?"

He shakes his head.

"She didn't kiss him."

Dahlia looks confused and before she can ask anymore questions, James gets there first.

"So, was there a happy ending?"

She claps her hands.

"Yes! Queen Mommy and Princess Dahlia baked cakes with the other princess and James the king taught daddy frog, lot's and lot's of tricks and they all built a great, big sandcastle to live in."

James feels warm inside as he thinks the 'other princess' might be the lady in her locket. His mother.

"Who's the other princess, love?"

He parks the car and waits for her reply.

"She's my sister princess."

Dahlia says, with a huge smile.

"But she's only little so Queen Mommy has to carry her everywhere."

His heart sinks.

He wondered how often Dahlia thought of having a sibling and then thinks about the amount of times, he wished that he and Jenny could give her one.

He unfastens her seatbelt and gets out to take her hand and lead her inside.

He opens the front door and waits there for a moment.

"Jennifer?"

In Her Shadow

He calls out.

"We are home, Dahlia's here."

He waits because he doesn't want to take Dahlia inside and have her find something, her poor little heart just couldn't handle.

"Jennifer?"

He calls again.

Jenny breezes down the hall to greet them.

She is wearing her favourite dress – a dress that James bought her, when they first started going out – and she wears a smile that doesn't seem fake or forced. She's happy.

"What are you just standing there for?"

She asks, pulling them in.

"Let's go see what's in the living room."

She winks at James, who lets go of Dahlia's hand so she can run in and see what Jenny has in store for her. He too, is curious.

He follows behind and as he enters the living room, he is amazed.

Jenny has – in the short time he was away – put together what looks like a kids party.

Complete with snacks, banners and two, neatly wrapped gifts; which sit on the coffee table.

One label reads 'Dahlia', while the other reads 'James'.

"What did you do?"

He asks in wonder, as Dahlia heads straight for the candy.

"We are having a party."

Jenny replies.

She picks up the gifts and hands them to them.

Dahlia's face lights up as she opens hers to find a doll - which eerily resembles Jenny - and she wraps her arms around it and squeezes.

"Thank you, mommy!"

In Her Shadow

She cries.
"She is the most beautiful doll in the whole, wide world!"
Jenny smiles and turns to James.
"Your turn."
She says, nodding to the gift.
He doesn't want to open his. He feels slightly embarrassed that he doesn't have anything to gift her in return and wants to wait until he has so it's equal but, she insists.
"Open it."
He gingerly tears at the wrapping and then slides it all off in one, to reveal a scrapbook.
His eyes glisten.
"Aw, love-"
"Look through it later."
She whispers.
"This is a party."
He pulls her into his arms and kisses her forehead and Dahlia watches, wondering why he looks so sad but she doesn't say anything. Instead, she plays with her dolly and Jenny goes to put some music on.
"Now, we can't have it too loud."
She says, with a mischievous grin.
"As, there is still one more guest to arrive and we need to hear the door."
She keeps the volume low.
"Who is it, mommy?"
"Yes, who is it, love? Who are we still waiting for?"
Jenny smiles and softens her eyes.
"You'll see."
James studies her face, trying to take from it any clues he can; on the mystery guest. He has nothing.
"Is it daddy?"
Asks Dahlia.

In Her Shadow

"No."

James and Jenny reply.

She is about to make another guess when the doorbell rings.

"Could you get that, baby?"

James eyes her suspiciously and goes to answer.

When he opens the door, he finds Richard. Jenny's dad.

"Happy birthday, son."

He says, handing James a card.

"It's not my-"

"It's only a little card. You read that later now, okay?"

He steps inside and waits for James to show him to the living room. James grows more and more confused as he shuffles his way back to the 'party'.

"Dad!"

Jenny cries, running to hug him.

"Come sit down."

She ushers him to the armchair and sits him down so that he is close to Dahlia, who looks at him in wonderment.

"Sweetheart, this is your granddad."

She says, taking her hand.

James' heart breaks as he takes in the scene.

First, Dahlia is cautious as she hugs Richard but then she is chatting away, showing him her doll and even offering him some candy.

It's a precious sight and Jenny manages to excuse herself for a second as she takes her place beside James, who is hovering close to the door.

"Sorry for springing this on you."

She whispers.

"I thought it was important that-"

"No apologies, love."

He says.

In Her Shadow

"This is beautiful."

She slips her hand into his and he almost forgets the card that he's holding in his other hand. Only, his fingertips have started to hurt as he was digging them tightly into it.

"So, your dad wished me a happy birthday and gave me this."

He holds out the card.

"That's weird, right?"

Jenny shakes her head.

"No. It's perfect."

He doesn't grasp her meaning.

"But it's not my birthday, love."

She smiles.

"It is, if you're just born..."

He raises his eyebrow.

"That's his way of accepting you."

She says.

"You're his son now."

James can't respond to this, he is too choked up.

He has never had a father before and although he believed he didn't need one, that didn't stop him from wanting one.

He is 38 years old and still longs for that father figure in his life. He couldn't find the words to describe how he was feeling now or to thank Jenny so instead, he kisses her.

He slides the card into his pocket, takes her face in his hands and crushes his lips against hers.

He is eternally grateful.

"James, look what granddad gave me?"

Dahlia tugs on his shirt and holds up her wrist to show him a little charm bracelet.

"Beautiful, love."

He says, and is reminded of the necklace in his pocket.

"Oh! Here, love. You're daddy said you were wanting to

wear this today."

He hands it to her.

"Maybe your granddad can help you put it on?"

He says, looking to Richard who is happy to oblige.

"Can I get you a tea or coffee, Richard?"

"Coffee please, son. Milk, no sugar."

James flashes a look at Jenny, finding this amusing.

"He's sweet enough."

She says.

James retreats to the kitchen, while Jenny sits with her father and daughter. He didn't want to get in the way, feeling they would be much better spending this time together without him so he decides; once he makes the coffee, he will find a way to excuse himself.

"Don't even try it."

He spins around and finds Jenny with an 'I know all' look, plastered on her face.

"What's that, love?"

He plays innocent.

"I could have made the coffee."

She says, leaning against the door frame.

"Yeah, I just thought-"

"Well, don't. This is your home."

He smiles.

"I know, love."

He sighs.

"Just thought it would be nice if you spent some time together as a family."

"And what are you, the neighbour's dog?"

She quips.

"You are family too, you know. I thought that was clear."

He reaches for the kettle and pours the boiling water into the cup, with the milk and coffee.

In Her Shadow

"No, it's clear."
He says, stirring the coffee.
"I just-"
She takes the cup from him.
"And it's appreciated but unnecessary."
She says, taking his hand with her free hand, to lead him back to the living room.
He follows. He wants to be there and he's glad that she wants him there too.
They sit on the sofa and Richard looks to them in awe, as he takes the cup from Jenny.
"You two are a nice fit."
He says, nodding his head.
James blushes as Jenny slips her hand in his.
"Thank you."
Richard smiles.
"I mean it. Never met a more suited pair."
Jenny mulls this over in her mind. Her father had only just met James and she wondered what granted such a statement.
"How so, dad?"
She asks.
"How are we suited?"
James starts to fidget beside her. He isn't sure if he wants to hear the answer because in raising this question, he doesn't know if Jenny is taking offence to the statement – so there was possible offence meant – or if she wasn't sure herself, why they fit. He is unsettled.
"It's in the eyes."
Says Richard, matter-of-factly.
"You look to each other to see who you truly are."
They both look at him, willing him to elaborate.
"Well, it's like this;"
He starts.

"If you aren't sure how you are coming across or if you need to know all the good things about yourselves, you look to each other."

He smiles again.

"You both know each other so well that you act as a mirror; holding up only the best things and that's all it takes for you both to feel good."

He continues.

"Just one look and you find in each other, the answers you have been looking for and that's really something special."

James lets this sink in. He found it strange that Richard could pick up on that, in such a short time of seeing them together and he wonders – but will never ask – why that wasn't the case, when Jenny was with William.

Why couldn't he see what William was doing to his little girl?

"You do love to talk, don't you, dad?"

Jenny giggles.

"I get it though. I know what you're saying."

Richard nods and he, Jenny and James, turn their attention to Dahlia.

She is eating some crisps and pretending to feed her doll some too.

"What are you going to call her, love?"

James asks.

"Lucy."

She replies, excitedly.

"She said she is enjoying the party and would like to dance now."

They all laugh.

They realise they have brought the 'party' down with too much conversation and they want Dahlia to have as much fun as she can so, they think up some party games and spend the rest of the evening laughing, playing and enjoying each other's company.

It was one of the more perfect nights, any of them had ever experienced.

As the night was coming to an end and Richard was leaving, he hugged Dahlia tight and Jenny even tighter; before turning to James.

"You too manly for a hug, son?"

James shakes his head and as he wraps his arms around Richard, he is overcome with emotion.

He had never felt the strong arms of a father, cradling him in warmth.

Jenny smiles wide as she watches them both; holding onto each other, longer than she expected them to and she feels at peace. That's one thing she didn't have to worry about anymore.

James wouldn't be alone when she was gone.

They wave Richard off and tuck Dahlia into bed and as Jenny falls asleep beside her; James steals himself away, to read the card that Richard gave him and look through the scrapbook from Jenny.

The card had a picture of a dolphin on the front and bold letters that read, 'keep swimming' and inside, he could just make out the handwriting as it was very small and seemed to be written, in a hurry.

It says;

"*James,*

I'm writing this as June sits in the other room. She still isn't thrilled about the visit the other day but I have faith, she will come around eventually. I know timing is crucial right now but trust me, it will happen.

I want to thank you for looking after my little girl, my heart. I can see she is very happy with you and the way you look at her; tells me that, she is more than a passing infatuation to you. You won't be letting her go easy and that's something we both have in common.

I'm sure we will find other things to bond over too.

Don't be a stranger. Whatever you need, don't be afraid or ashamed to ask.

I always wanted a son,
Richard."

James reads the card two more times, before closing it and placing it on the coffee table.

He sniffs back some tears and as if his heart were an anchor, it sinks deeper into the ocean of his chest.

He thinks about leaving the scrapbook for another day. A day where he feels less weighed down with his sorrow but he couldn't do that to Jenny.

She wanted him to look at it after the party and so he will.

He takes a deep breath and with a shaky hand, turns to the first page.

A photograph of he and Jenny has been glued to the centre of the page and around it; she has written things like, 'You're eyes are so green' and 'I just love your accent'. Words – he remembers – that were exchanged during their first date.

He is saddened as he recounts that time himself. He remembers how full of energy Jenny was; keeping the conversation flowing all night and how captivated he was by her every, little movement.

He loved the way her nose crinkled when she laughed and the way she licked her lips after every sip of her drink.

Never a believer in love at first sight, she made a believer of him that night as he fell head over heels for her, on the spot. He couldn't believe how long ago it seemed and yet, how brief it felt at the same time.

He decides to leave the rest until another night and retires to bed; Where he hoped to carry that night with him, as he

In Her Shadow

slipped into a dream.

Chapter 14: The Dress

"I don't know. This one makes me look too pale."

It's three days later and Jenny is trying on wedding dresses as her big day — it had been decided - was just around the corner.

"Well..."

Says the shop assistant.

"You are getting married in black and that's a colour that would make anyone look..."

She pauses to find the right phrase.

"washed out."

She decides.

Jenny rolls her eyes.

"What happened to 'black goes with everything'?"

She asks, huffily.

"And 'every woman should have a little, black dress'?"

The lady shrugs and shakes her head.

"I didn't write that book, I don't know."

Jenny sighs.

"Why don't you try the backless one again? I don't think that was as dark as this one."

The lady offers.

"I..."

Jenny tries to think of an excuse, not wanting to admit the truth. That dress hung off of her body, revealing that she had lost even more weight and she knew that nobody would want to see her spine; jutting out at them, as she walked down the aisle.

"I don't think that's 'the dress'."

She says, smiling at the lady.

In Her Shadow

The shop assistant smiles back. She doesn't know of Jenny's illness but she detects that there is an urgency – something beyond the usual urgency – to find the perfect dress for her big day and as she was pleasant enough, she was going to help her as much as she could.

"Have you thought about how you are going to accessorize?"

She asks, looking to Jenny's feet.

Jenny hadn't really thought about that. Her sole focus was; finding a dress that didn't make her look 'half dead' and marrying the man she loved. She didn't have the time to think about what kind of shoes or jewellery she would do it in.

"I haven't..."

She sighs.

"What goes best with black?"

The lady laughs.

"Black goes with everything."

Jenny laughs too.

"Then, I'll have everything from Yellow, to red."

She shakes off the dress she is wearing and takes a long look at herself as she stands in her underwear.

She used to complain that she was 'flabby' and dimpled in places, where she believed she shouldn't be dimpled. She wanted the dimples on the bottom of her back – the way toned backs were dimpled – and she wanted to feel the bones in her hips; instead of the soft, sponginess.

James would always drop kisses on all of the places that made her insecure the most and he would tell her how beautiful she was and she never once believed him.

The body that she is looking at now; she couldn't imagine him kissing those same places and complimenting her, the way he did before.

Running her hands over the bony places, she didn't feel

happy. This wasn't the toned body she always dreamed of. She was bordering skeletal and she imagined how uncomfortable it must've felt to hug her and longed to have her 'podgy' body again.

The shop assistant watches her and she feels a lump rise in her throat as she takes in the sadness on Jenny's face. She didn't want to speculate but she couldn't help it; she guessed that the woman in front of her was sick – dying maybe – and needed to find a dress that would make her feel beautiful for the last time.

She clears her throat.

"I think ruffles and layers are coming back."

She says, feeling this type of dress would be better, for a frame like Jenny's.

"Not so many people are into the figure hugging dresses these days as they enjoy the flamboyancy... would you like me to look out some of those kinds of dresses?"

Jenny collects herself and smiles at the kind lady.

"Yes... thank you."

She nods.

"I think something like that would be perfect."

The lady scurries away and when she returns; she has with her, only one dress.

Jenny thinks this is due to it being heavy. Maybe one was all the lady could carry but the shop assistant grins.

"I think you would look amazing in this."

Jenny is sceptical. She doesn't believe that she will look amazing in anything again but she doesn't want to hurt the lady's feelings and agrees to try it on.

She turns her back to the mirror and lets the lady button her up. The material doesn't feel as heavy as she thought it would and instead, it feels great against her skin. She wants to steal a glimpse in the mirror but she decides to wait until the dress is sitting as it should, so she can give it a fair chance.

"There. I knew this would look amazing."

Says the shop assistant.

Jenny turns slowly and when she looks in the mirror, she is stunned.

"I- I-"

"You're beautiful!"

The lady exclaims.

Jenny wanted to disbelieve her but she was finding it hard. She not only felt it but the mirror showed that she looked it too.

This was the dress.

"How did you do that?"

Jenny asks, in amazement.

"Do what?"

"The dress. How did you know it would be the one?"

The lady smiles.

"It's my job. I'm supposed to 'just know'."

Jenny is close to tears. .

"Isn't there anyone you would like to call, dear?"

The lady asks.

"Someone who can enjoy this moment with you?"

Jenny looks to her feet.

"I know it's not traditional for me to wear black but, I'm keeping the tradition of it being bad luck for James – the man I'm marrying – to see me in the dress."

She says, embarrassed that she doesn't have anyone. It's not like the movies for her at all; where the mother goes along, with a few close friends. Jenny only had James to rely on and she didn't want Dahlia to share this moment. She knew it would be difficult to keep it together and so, it was best to do this alone.

"I see."

The woman feels even more sorry for her.
"Best to surprise everyone on the day anyway, eh?"
She smiles and Jenny nods.
"So, this is definitely the one you want?"
"Oh yes! No doubt. It even fits perfectly."

They share another smile and the woman exits the changing room, to give Jenny some privacy to take the dress off.

Both of them are in their element and before Jenny leaves the store, she squeezes the woman tight and thanks her copiously.

She steps outside and reaches for her phone to call a taxi but before she can get the chance to dial the number, James pulls up in his car and beeps his horn.

"Do you need a lift, ma'am?"
He calls out, pretending he doesn't know her.
"I don't get in cars with strange men."
She says, playing along.
"Who you calling strange?"
He steps out of the car and holds the passenger door open for her.
"Heard it's gonna rain, love."
He says, peering up at the sky.
"Strange or not, I'll keep you warm."
Jenny smiles and gets inside.
"I found it."
She says, fastening her seatbelt.
"Found...?"
He replies.
"The dress. I found the dress."
He smiles.
"That's fantastic, love. Did you take a picture?"
"What do you mean, did I take a picture?"
"To show me."

In Her Shadow

Jenny tuts.

"Have you no clue? It's bad luck."

James nods. He didn't think there was anything worse than what they were currently dealing with so; he thought seeing her in the dress, would be a good thing.

"I get it, love."

He says.

"It'll be more special to wait anyway."

They both smile.

It starts to rain as they drive home and Jenny watches as the raindrops slide slowly and then quickly, down the windscreen.

She has always loved the rain and how relaxing it felt to just watch the little drops as they fell together and formed puddles.

She imagines them as tiny people, falling from the sky and the puddles are the new homes that they built.

"James?"

He drives on.

"Yes, love?"

"Do you believe in heaven?"

Her question takes him by surprise and he tries not to slow the car down but, he is finding it hard to keep going and ponder this thought at the same time.

He pulls into a street – that isn't far from their own – and parks.

"Do you?"

He asks her.

"I asked you first."

She says, looking at him from the side of her eye.

"Do you believe in heaven?"

James isn't a religious man and Jenny is a believer to an extent so he didn't know if he should tell her his true thoughts, or give her an answer that would wrap her up in a little bubble and keep her happy.

He always wanted to keep her happy.

"I believe heaven exists, if you believe it does."

He says, going for what he thought was a safe answer.

"So, we are working with the power of belief and not hard facts?"

She replies, not satisfied with this answer.

"What do you believe?"

He asks.

"I believe there is a heaven."

She replies.

"Then, there is, love."

He says, with a smile.

"Because I believe there is?"

James turns slightly, to look at her.

"Yes, that makes it real to you."

He says.

"But not to you?"

She asks.

He doesn't know where this is heading.

"If there is a heaven, love and angels are real?"

He smiles.

"I know there will definitely be a place for you there."

She frowns.

"And if there isn't? If heaven doesn't exist?"

"Then you make your own?"

He offers.

Jenny isn't ready to drop it yet. She desperately needed to know there was a heaven, that there is some place beyond this and that there isn't really an end.

"How will you find me?"

She asks, in a whisper.

"If I believe in heaven and I go there and you don't believe there is one, how will you find me?"

James grips the steering wheel; trying to hold every little bit of hurt he feels, tight inside him.

"I will always find you, Jennifer..."

She covers his hand – which is digging tighter and tighter into the wheel, causing his knuckles to turn white – with her cold, trembling hand and squeezes.

"Let's go home."

She says, letting it go.

"It's cold."

James nods slowly and proceeds to take them home.

Once inside; Jenny runs to the bathroom and James is about to continue on to the living room, when he hears her retching.

He leans against the wall.

"Are you okay, love?"

She retches again.

"Do you want me to hold your hair back?"

She doesn't reply. She didn't want him to see her this way; she didn't even like to sneeze in front of James because he always made a fuss over her and tried to nurse her back to health, as best he could.

He knocks on the door lightly.

"Love, I'm coming in."

She is about to lock the door but once again, she needs to vomit.

He cautiously steps inside and gathers her hair up with a shaky hand and rubs her back with the other.

She is comforted by his touch but embarrassed that he has to see this.

"It's okay, love."

He soothes.

"Best to get it all up."

He puts his arm around her now and kisses her shoulder.
"I'm here. It's okay."
She sinks into him and slowly crumbles and he moves with her; until they are sitting on the floor.
"Do you want to go to bed, love?"
He asks, empathetic.
"You must be really tired."
She nods and rests her head against his chest.
"Right. I'm just going to stand now and help you up, okay?"
He moves slowly and carefully as he helps her to her feet.
Jenny steadies herself and pulls away.
"I'm just going to brush my teeth first."
She says, mortified about the smell of sick.
"Okay, love."
He steps back outside the toilet, giving her some space and waits.
"James..."
His ears prick up at the sound of her voice.
"Yes, love?"
He waits.
"I can't get up."
He steps back inside once more and finds her sitting on the toilet seat. She hangs her head in embarrassment but James doesn't pick up on it. He thinks she is just too weak to look at him.
"Does it hurt?"
He asks, wishing he could suffer it all for her.
"Yes."
She responds.
"Where?"
He wanted to know where was okay for him to apply pressure and where it would hurt her so he could avoid that.
"Everywhere."

In Her Shadow

She breathes.

"Right..."

He tries to be as gentle as he can as he drapes her arm around his neck and scoops her up; cradling her like a newborn.

He carries her upstairs and eases her onto their bed.

They don't say anything as he begins to slip her shoes and socks off and as he starts to undress her, to help her on with her pyjamas; Jenny's heart sinks. She didn't want him to see.

"You don't have-"

"I do."

He says, cutting her off.

"More than that, I want to."

He decides it's easier if she wears a nightgown instead and before he slips it over her head – to cover her body – he let's his eyes soak up her fragile frame.

It's hard for him to come to terms with – seeing her look so weak and tired – but she is still just as beautiful to him, as she was when they first met.

"Yours is the skin I love the most."

He says, planting a kiss on her collarbone, which is much more prominent than he remembers.

"Even the moon cries because her skin isn't as soft and transcendent as yours."

He pulls her nightgown down and catches her smile.

"Rest well, love."

He tucks her in and strokes her hair as she closes her eyes and drifts into a dream.

"Don't go too far."

He whispers, and exits the room.

Downstairs now, he retrieves the scrapbook that Jenny put together for him and sits, nestling it in his lap.

On page two, he finds a poem.

In Her Shadow

"There is a man I call 'my shadow'
but he doesn't look a thing like me.
His hands are rough but his heart is soft
and his mouth is like a snowflake.
That's not to say that it's cold and icy
I mean to say it is unique,
from it; the most beautiful words flow
words no one, has ever said to me.
I think he's an angel."

The last line reminds James of their conversation in the car and suddenly, he finds himself wishing there was a heaven. There had to be somewhere where they could meet again, where eternity exists. If 'heaven' – he thought – was that place, he would convert to every religion to get there.

He closes the book, deciding to only take in one page at a time and when he needed to see them most.

Closing his eyes, he doesn't mean to fall asleep but the Sandman comes for him and he dreams away on the sofa.

Chapter 15: Superman

"Baby...Baby..."

James opens his eyes to find Jenny standing before him.

She looks less tired than she did when he last looked at her and she's smiling from ear to ear.

"Why don't you go upstairs?"

She coaxes.

"That sofa always hurts your back."

He gathers his thoughts. He doesn't remember falling asleep and wonders how long he had been down there for, how long he had been away from Jenny's side.

"What time is it, love?"

He asks, groggily.

"It's 6:30. Guess the alarm is working today."

He gives himself a shake.

"Aw, love! I meant to switch-"

"If you switched it off, I would be late."

He tilts his head to the side.

"Late?"

He asks, wondering where she is going.

"For work."

He sinks back into the sofa. Wondering if maybe he is dreaming and that Jenny is still sound asleep upstairs.

"You're not well enough, love."

She giggles.

"I'm absolutely fine. Come on, go to bed."

She goes to take his hand and he pulls it away.

"I'm fine."

She sits beside him.

"I want to go in today, James."

He clenches his jaw. He never stood in the way of anything she wanted to do but he had the urge, to do that today.

"Are you sure, love?"

He asks.

"I mean-"

"Won't change my mind."

That was him told.

He nods.

"Right. Well, I will come with you."

She shakes her head.

"Actually..."

She treads carefully.

"I kind of have a little favour to ask."

James listens.

"Well, you know I told William to shop for a dress with Dahlia because it would be too hard for me?"

He nods.

"She's been asking-"

"Aw, Jennifer, don't."

He presses his fingertips to his temples.

"I wouldn't ask and it's not my wish but-"

"I know. I know, love and I want her to have a good day too but please, it can't be that."

She squeezes his knee.

"I'm afraid it is."

He sighs heavily.

"And this favour?"

He asks.

"I was wondering if you would ask him."

This knocks James off kilter.

Jenny knows he would do anything for her and this was no

exception but it hurt him still, that she was asking.

He takes her hand.

"When?"

He asks, trying not to show the hurt.

"When I leave for the diner. I can text him to come over."

"Right. I'll drop you off first."

She stands.

"No, I want to walk in today. It's an okay day."

She goes to get ready and James remains seated. He is happy to see her feeling better and in high spirits, which is a drastic change from yesterday. He focuses on that.

When she returns, she has that wide smile on her face once more.

"How do I look?"

He stands and takes both of her hands in his.

"Radiant, love."

He says, forcing a smile.

She grins and leans in for a kiss and as they pull their lips away from each other, only one mouth remains smiling; Jenny's.

"At least let me pick you up at the end of your shift?"

Jenny nods.

"Deal."

With that, she flutters out of the door and on to the street.

James watches her from the window until she is out of sight and then goes to get ready, before William comes around.

The doorbell rings.

William nods at James.

"James."

He says.

"William."

James steps aside and lets him in.

They walk up the hall awkwardly; before taking a seat opposite each other in the living room.

"How's Jen?"

James hates this. He doesn't want to waste any time on this man and he doesn't like him asking after Jenny, like he cares about her. He doesn't – James thinks – care an ounce.

"She's fine."

He replies, clenching his jaw.

"Good."

They nod.

"So, what's Dahlia's dress like?"

"Why, you looking to get one in your size?"

William jokes, but it isn't received well.

"It's purple. Her favourite colour."

James snorts.

"Her favourite colour is blue, mate."

He says.

"So you know my daughter better than I do?"

William asks, affronted.

"Didn't say that."

They scowl at each other.

"What's this about anyway?"

William huffs, and James forgets the matter at hand.

"What?"

He asks.

"Why am I here?"

James remembers.

"Dr. Frankenstein needed a new project?"

He jokes.

"Ha Ha, almost bust a rib with that one there."

William says sarcastically.

"And anyway, if you were trying to insult me by calling me a monster; you could've at least picked one that didn't derive empathy from the viewers."

"Right enough."

Says James, nodding.

"No one will be feeling sorry for someone like you anytime soon."

William rolls his eyes.

"So we can't all be heroes."

He says.

"Is this why you brought me here? Have you developed some Messiah complex and want to save me or something?"

James laughs.

"Wouldn't spit on you if you were perishing in flames, mate."

William nods.

"Likewise."

They draw each other a disgusted look and James bites the bullet.

"Dahlia wants you at the wedding."

He sighs.

"I don't, Jenny doesn't but that little girl does and-"

"I'll tell her I'm busy."

James smirks.

"You've more willpower than me, mate. She could ask me to jump off the Chrysler building and I'd do it so I wouldn't have to tell her no."

"Pity you don't just do that anyway."

James clenches his jaw at this.

"What inconvenience do I cause you anyway, William? Why don't you want me around?"

William narrows his eyes.

"Can ask you the same thing."

"No you can't."

"Why's that?"

James bites his lip.

"Well, you upset Jennifer and that upsets – and inconveniences – me. I love Jennifer, would never hurt her and I care about your daughter a great deal. I'm not the bad guy here."

William considers this.

"You're her guy though and that makes you the bad guy to me."

He admits.

"You're the main antagonist in my story whereas; you are the hero in hers."

James hangs his head.

"Yeah... but heroes save lives..."

He says, with a heavy heart.

They both let this statement hang in the air. Jenny's life couldn't be saved and in the end, neither of them will get the girl and the happily ever after. Hero or villain; they were fighting against the same evil. The cancer.

"Coffee?"

Offers James, after a long five minutes.

"No."

Says William.

"I'm leaving in a minute."

James shrugs.

"Suit yourself."

William huffs.

"Is it really blue?"

"What?"

"Dahlia's favourite colour. Is it really blue?"

James nods.

"I'll return the purple one. I would have taken her with me but-"

"You were supposed to. She's supposed to pick her own

dress."

William nods.

"She will."

He stands up and extends his hand to James.

"I'm not asking you to be my friend, James but can we squash everything? Can we forget it for now?"

James hesitates but then shakes his hand.

"For now."

He sees William out and when he leaves; he pulls his jacket on and sets out to the diner. He wanted to tell Jenny that it was all under control, that things would be okay but also, he wanted to make sure she was still feeling well enough to do her shift.

Making his way towards the counter, Jenny doesn't see him coming.

"I'd like to order a kiss, with a side of hand holding and an 'I love you' for dessert, please?"

Jenny looks up and smiles.

"Sorry, sir, what menu are you reading from?"

He leans in and steals a kiss.

"The one that doesn't come with prices... what would you call it... priceless?"

She giggles.

He still had the power to send a sea of butterflies crashing through her tummy and dimples to her cheeks, as she smiled an ever growing smile.

"Ah, that would be our secret menu, sir."

She says, winking at him.

"Take a seat and I will see what I can do."

He sits on one of the counter stools and takes her hands.

"I love you."

He says.

"I love you too."

She replies.

Before they can say anything else, customers start to appear.

"No rest for the wicked."

She sighs.

"Well, you better take a seat and I'll get these orders."

He replies, placing his fingers to his forehead, to make 'devil horns'.

Jenny doesn't argue. She is actually glad of the break and lets him take over as she takes the seat he was sitting in.

She watches him as he takes the orders. She never really noticed before but he was amazing with the customers; very charming but professional at the same time.

"You're better than me at this."

She says.

"Never, love."

After he has made sure every customer is satisfied, he steals a moment to chat with Jenny again.

"Has it been busy?"

"Not really."

He smiles.

"You amaze me, you do."

She smiles back.

"Why's that?"

"You just keep on keeping on and don't let anything get you down."

She nods.

She was falling apart just as much as he was but, she never wanted him to know that.

"Did William show?"

James wanted to forget all about him.

"Yeah. He said he will tell Dahlia he is busy."

Jenny closes her eyes and sighs.

"He has to come, James."

"But why, Jennifer?"

She opens her eyes and looks into his.

"It's what Dahlia wants."

He wasn't going to debate this with her. He would give Dahlia the moon if he could but he didn't understand why Jenny wasn't so reluctant, in agreeing that he could come. He thought William would be the last person she wanted there.

Jenny taps into his thoughts.

"Maybe I want to rub it in. Maybe I want him to sit and watch, as I marry the man he could never be."

She thought this would make James feel better but it only troubled him further. That wasn't why he was marrying her.

He wanted the day to be about their love and their commitment to each other.

William had already had his wedding day with Jenny; this one didn't need to be about him too.

"You're not that spiteful, love. I know it's all for Dahlia and that's more than okay with me."

He lies.

For the rest of the shift, Jenny remains seated and James serves the customers and cleans up after them.

She remembers a time she used to call him her Clark Kent and she, his Lois Lane. Looking at him now, she deems him her 'Superman'. He doesn't – and never did – wear any disguises.

He was the real deal; the bird and the plane. He was made of steel.

"James?"

He stops.

"Yes, love?"

She smiles warmly.

"You're going to be just fine."

He doesn't need to ask her what she means by this. He knows she meant when she was gone, he will be okay but what he didn't know was; how could she think that?

He was barely hanging on as it was and that was with her sitting in front of him.

He fakes a smile in response and continues cleaning up.

There wasn't much conversation on the journey home and as they stepped through their front door, it was like stepping into another world.

The atmosphere around them felt strange and nothing seemed to be in the right place. They both felt it. Their once happy – and together – home, was starting to dismantle with melancholy.

It just isn't fair, they think.

Chapter 16: Milk, Two Sugars

"So this was her dream? To serve food from a shanty?"

It's a dreary afternoon and the diner is near empty and as James looks up to see who has just spoken these words, he is surprised to see Jenny's mother.

"June, Mrs -"

He stops, not knowing her last name.

"June is fine."

She doesn't hide the fact that she is looking down her nose at him.

"Some dream."

She says, her face scrunched up; like she has just encountered a bad smell..

James is embarrassed. He's the one who bought this place for Jenny and tried to fix it up as best he could. It was all he could afford.

"Jennifer is at home today."

He says, hoping this would make her want to leave.

June purses her lips.

"Then I'll just have to make do with you."

She sighs.

"Coffee, when you're ready...Jason, is it?"

She says, pretending she doesn't remember his name.

"James."

He replies, slightly irritated.

"Milk, two sugars."

She says.

He jokes to himself that she is bitter and in need of the

sugar; but he doesn't say anything insulting out loud. He wants to keep the peace, for Jenny's sake.

"No problem."

He nods.

June takes a seat at the counter and watches him. He seems smaller than she remembered, more mouse like. Timid.

"And my daughter isn't here because?"

He places her coffee in front of her.

"She needs the rest."

He replies.

"And you're here why?"

He starts cleaning the counter nervously.

"We need the money."

She chuckles.

"Should have taken the envelope."

She says. "We make our own money, ma'am."

June doesn't like this. She is not used to being talked back to.

"Yes, I can see business is booming." She says, sarcastically.

"We do okay."

He says, still cleaning.

"What if it was here now?"

He looks up.

"What?"

He asks, unsure of what she means.

"The envelope."

She smiles a wicked smile; that would make Cruella, shake out of her fur coat.

"What if it was only offered to you?"

James is affronted.

"Are you seriously trying to do this?"

In Her Shadow

She laughs.
"I didn't hear a 'no' in there."
He slams the cloth on the counter.
"Get out."
June doesn't budge.
"I will when I finish my coffee but first, tell me this, how are you planning on paying for her funeral?"
James has to hold on to the counter. His legs have suddenly lost the ability to hold him up.
"June I-"
She takes out the envelope that was rejected previously.
"Does it look tempting now?"
He doesn't even look at it.
"We make our own money."
She sets it down.
"Enough to cover the expenses of-
"Enough."
He says, not letting her finish.
She shrugs.
"What about Dahlia?"
James narrows his eyes.
"What about her?"
"Is there enough for her?"
He nods.
"I will still be working here and William-"
"William can't even make a sandwich, never mind enough money to look after that little girl, Jason."
"James."
"I don't care."
She stands.
"He would take the envelope in a heartbeat."
She shouts.
"Why won't you?"

He looks her dead in the eye.

"There's a lot of things that he would do, that I wouldn't even dream of."

He says, calmly.

"I am not him."

June sits again.

"No, you're not."

She huffs.

"That doesn't mean I'll ever like you though."

James rolls his eyes.

"This isn't about you liking me, June. You don't have to like me."

He leans towards her.

"This is about spending the time you have left. Not your money."

He pushes the envelope away from him.

"You can keep that."

June keeps her expression stony but deep down; there lies a heart that hurts, just as much as James' did.

She nods.

"I know Richard came to see you both."

She says, putting the envelope away.

"He did, yeah. Dahlia was so happy."

June is caught by surprise.

"She saw him? Dahlia was there?"

James didn't know that June wasn't aware of this part.

He drops his head.

"You're more than welcome at ours too, you know."

He says.

"Our door is always open."

She lets this sink in. She didn't want to miss out on anymore of her granddaughter's life but she didn't feel comfortable, just turning up at their home.

In Her Shadow

"And Jennifer?"

She wonders.

"She will just let me see her?"

James nods.

"She came to you, June, she got in touch. She didn't do that so you could turn her away and vice versa."

She runs her eyes over him once more. This time, she doesn't feel contempt for the man she sees before her and instead; she is thankful.

"You've really done right by her, haven't you, James?"

He sighs.

"I've tried."

"And this place?"

She asks, taking another look around.

"A gift from you?"

He nods.

"It didn't look like this when we got it, you know."

He throws a quick look around too.

"This is the progress so far and it's only going to get better."

June smiles.

"Thank you."

She says.

"Thank you for making her dreams come true."

James isn't sure what to say. It was only a diner but June could care less about that. She knew the main dream that her daughter chased; was that of a happy life and he had given her that, in the short time they had been together.

She sees that now.

"When will you have Dahlia again?"

She asks.

"I'd like to see her."

James smiles wide.

"When would you like to see her?"
"Soon."
She replies.
"Very soon."
She sips what is left of her coffee and stands to leave.

Before she goes, James comes around the counter and stands in front of her.

"Is it too much to ask for a hug?"
He enquires.
"Are we 'there' yet?"

June looks to her feet and before she can give her answer; she feels James' arms, wrap themselves around her.

She is warmed by his embrace but she doesn't hug him back.

June isn't 'there' yet.

"Thank you."
He whispers in her ear.
"A million times, thank you."

She has nothing left to say. She hurries off, leaving James standing taller than before. He is elated. He knew this was important to Jenny and June would regret it if she never got to mend fences with her.

This was a good day.

He decides to close the diner early. He wants to rush home to tell Jenny the news – that her mother wants to visit – but before he does this, he drops into a local shop and buys her the biggest bunch of flowers they have.

"Hello, most beautiful girl in the world."
He says, handing her the flowers and kissing her on the forehead.

"Got something to tell you."
Jenny tuts.
"What did you get me these for?"

She says, letting them hang limp in her hand.
"Do you not see what you are gifting me?"
He is taken aback at the tone of her voice.
"I thought they'd bring a little colour to the place, love and-"
"They die."
She says, frostily.
"You've given me something that's just going to shrivel up and die. That's very inappropriate, don't you think?"
He really didn't think of it this way and he is mortified that Jenny has.
"I didn't mean-"
"Yeah well, you've done it now."
She huffs.
"I may as well find a vase for them."
She exits the room and James is left helpless. He knows that what she is saying, isn't really meant and he tries to not let it affect him. It does though. It cuts him deep.
Jenny returns, without the flowers.
"Left them in the kitchen."
She says.
"I don't want them sitting in here."
James nods.
"I understand, love."
She tuts again.
"I'm afraid – Mr. know it all – you know nothing at all."
She glues her hands to her hips and gives him and icy stare.
"What was it you were shouting about anyway?"
James sighs.
"I didn't realise I was shouting, love. I'm sorry."
Jenny's mood shifts suddenly, as she takes in the look on his face and her heart squeezes.
"James... I..."

He sniffs back some tears.
"I know, love. I know."
She throws herself into his arms and kisses his face all over.
"You don't deserve this…"
He clings to her and lets the tears fall.
It was she – he thought to himself – who didn't deserve this and if he could take it all for her, he would. She knew this.
"They're beautiful, they're my favourite flowers."
She says, catching his tears with a bony finger.
"I'll bring them in."
She tries to go and get them but he won't let her go. He squeezes and squeezes her as he sobs, softly into her shoulder.
She strokes his hair.
"It'll all be okay."
She says, not quite believing it herself.
"You can do this."

Chapter 17: Salt In The Woods

Jenny sits on the sofa; waiting for William to drop Dahlia off and James sits in the armchair, watching her twist her fingers through her hair.

"You nervous, love?"

He asks, his knee twitching slightly. He was quite nervous himself.

Jenny looks at him and shakes her head.

"I just wish he would hurry up, before my mom gets here. I don't want them around at the same time."

James nods.

"I under-"

The sound of the doorbell renders him silent and they both look at each other, not sure who should answer.

The doorbell rings again.

"I'll get it, love."

James makes his way down the hall, palms sweaty and thoughts scattered. He wants this day to go well for Jenny but he has a sinking feeling in his stomach, that tells him; it just might not.

He opens the door.

"June, come in."

He says, loudly so Jenny can hear who it is.

"Dahlia isn't here yet but Jennifer is in the living room."

June hesitantly makes her way up the hall and James follows, wishing the doorbell would ring again so he could skip the awkward scene; he knew was about to take place.

"Hello, mom."

Jenny doesn't rise from the sofa and June hovers in the doorway.

"Jennifer, you're looking well."

Jenny rolls her eyes.

"Do you need to be somewhere?"

She asks, tutting.

June looks confused.

"No. I made sure I was free all day, to see Dahlia."

She replies.

Jenny motions to the armchair.

"So why are you standing half in, half out the door, mom? Take a seat, for God's sake."

Her snappiness startles June but she obliges.

"Will I put the kettle on, love?"

James asks, looking for any escape.

"Two sugars, June?"

"Nothing for me."

She replies.

"Or me."

Jenny seconds.

"Right then... I'll go check and see if Dahlia's here yet?"

Jenny huffs.

"Sit down, James. She will be here when she's here."

James sits beside her but not as close as he usually would.

"I know, love. Just excited is all."

She huffs again.

"No, you just don't want to be here, James."

She looks to June.

"And I don't want you here just as much as you don't want to be here, mom."

She says, scowling.

June is offended.

"I do want to be here, Jennifer. Dahlia is important to me."

In Her Shadow

Jenny stands.

"So important that you abandon her mother and only come running; when you know that I won't be around for much longer, to throw that fact in your face!"

She storms out.

James sits open mouthed. He didn't see this outburst coming at all and isn't quite sure how to handle it.

"It's not her, June. It's-"

"No, it is. She has every right, it's okay."

He stands.

"I'll only be a minute"

He says, knowing he must go after Jenny.

"Are you sure you don't want a coffee?"

She shakes her head.

"She needs you."

He exits the living room in search of Jenny and finds her, sitting on the steps outside their front door.

"Room for me there, love?"

She tuts and makes some space.

"It's cold out here."

He says, squeezing in beside her.

"Then go back inside."

She sighs.

He puts his arm around her and pulls her into him.

"You want to talk about it, love?"

She clasps her hands and rests them on his knee.

"It just hurts."

She says, shrugging.

"She's only here to see Dahlia but what about me, James? Where's my sorry? My – My"

She can't say the rest and James squeezes her tight.

"What about your father, love?"

Jenny doesn't understand his question.

"What about him?"
"He disowned you too and he-"
"It's different with him."
She pulls away.
"Look at it this way; if I told you not to talk to someone, would you still talk to them?"
He shakes his head.
"No, but-"
"Well, it's like you."
She says.
"You'd do anything for me because you love me, yes?"
He nods.
"Yes, but-"
"Then, that's just like my dad. He loves my mom and whatever she says goes."
James takes her hands.
"But..."
He starts.
"If it were a matter of not speaking to my child – who I also love – there would be no contest, love. A father's love for his child has to rule over that, of the love for his partner."
Jenny shakes her head.
"But, James-"
"See it this way, love;"
He interjects.
"I never knew my father because he walked out on us but you did. You knew who yours was and you loved him and he you and yet-"
"And yet he washed his hands of me."
She says, shaking her head.
"But he tried to make up for it, did he not?"
James nods.
"Yes, love. Now it's your mum's turn."

He squeezes her hands.

"I'm not saying you have to go in there and act like what she – what they – did doesn't matter."

He says.

"You don't have to do that but think of Dahlia. Today is about her and it hurts me too that it can't be about you also but, I think it would hurt you more if you didn't let them spend some time together."

Jenny nods. She agrees with him. She knows it would hurt her; if she deprived Dahlia of a grandmother and she didn't want to carry that hurt with her, until the very end.

"I'm ready."

She says, getting to her feet.

"You were born ready, love."

He encourages.

They walk back to the living room and take a seat. This time, James leaves no space between he and Jenny. He makes sure she can feel him; sturdy by her side, if she needed to lean on him at any moment.

"Not here yet?"

June asks.

"She shouldn't be too long."

James replies.

"Will isn't good with timekeeping, is he, love? You tell him be here in an hour and he hears two hours, eh love?"

He nudges Jenny.

"Mmm."

She sighs.

"Actually, James, I think I will have that coffee. I'm a little bit parched."

Says June.

James looks to Jenny who nods, letting him know that it is okay to leave her there.

"Right. I'll be back in a minute." He says, and this time; he doesn't want to escape. He wanted to stay by Jenny's side.

As soon as he exits the room, Jenny leans forward to June and brings her voice to a whisper.

"You were never my mother."

She hisses.

"And you were an even worse wife!"

June drops her jaw.

"Jennifer I-"

Jenny throws her hand up in a 'stop' motion.

"I know what you did."

She says, her eyes flashing.

"You thought you hid it well but I always knew."

June doesn't try to deny what Jenny thinks she knows. She has been caught out.

"And your dad?"

She asks, afraid of the answer.

"Does he know?"

Jenny chuckles.

"Of course. Why do you think he went along with it, when you told him not to speak to any of us? Did you think it was because he hated me?"

She snorts.

"He didn't think I knew. He wanted me to be happy and live in blissful ignorance but more than that, he didn't want his wife stepping out on him again."

She grinds her teeth.

"Especially, with his daughter's fiancé."

June purses her lips.

"And yet you married him."

She says.

"I was so young and pregnant with his kid, mom!"

Jenny replies, raising her voice.

"What did I know about raising a baby alone? I never learned anything from you!"

James overhears this and comes back to the living room.

"Everything okay?"

He asks concerned.

"No."

Jenny replies.

"Everything is as it always was. Messed up."

James places June's coffee in front of her and takes his seat beside Jenny again.

"Love, Dahlia will be here soon and-"

Jenny laughs.

"You want in on the secret, James?"

She asks, not caring about anyone knowing now. She has kept it to herself for so long; suffered in silence, but not now. She wasn't dying, without unmasking her mother; revealing the monster, she truly is.

"You want to know why I can't stand this woman?"

James sighs.

"Love, don't-"

"No! Don't you."

She snaps.

"Don't you defend her. You don't know what she did."

June sits in silence.

"What's wrong, Junie? That's what he called you, wasn't it, 'Junie'? You upset 'cause this one only has eyes for me?"

James Squeezes her shoulder.

"Jennifer-"

"She slept with William, James."

James is flabbergasted as the problem becomes clear. He can't quite believe what he is hearing.

"Not only that."

Jenny continues.

"She's the reason he raised his hands to me. He left bruises on me – bruises you saw, James. Remember? – even when we weren't together and why? Why did he do that?"

She clenches her jaw.

"Because he couldn't hit his little 'Junie'. Oh no, she was too precious but the woman who was carrying – who birthed – his baby, wasn't. I was the punch bag."

She starts to shake.

"You made him hate me."

She points to June.

"You wanted him all to yourself and you didn't care what that would mean for me."

James pulls her in close to him and lets her cry it out.

"I think you better leave, June."

His voice is shaking but he means what he says.

"You aren't welcome here at all."

June takes a deep breath.

"I just want to see my granddaughter, James. You must understand I-"

"Get out."

He orders.

"Now."

She jumps to her feet, as if an electric shock has just shot through her seat and exits their home.

Jenny can't stop crying and tears start to spill from James' eyes too. He understands now that there is no going back with Jenny's mother. She had betrayed her daughter in one of the worst ways he could think of and that's not someone – although it wasn't his call – he wanted around Dahlia.

"I'm sorry."

He whispers.

Jenny pulls away from him and stares at him in

bewilderment.

"You're sorry?"

She sniffs.

"You never have to say that to me. You never apologise, okay?"

He hangs his head.

"I didn't know, love I-"
"Because I didn't tell you."

She says.

"My dad is a good man."

James nods.

"A great man."

He says, thinking about what torment he must've went through also.

They dry their tears and try to figure out what they will tell Dahlia. She knew she was coming here today to meet her grandmother but that just couldn't happen now. Then there was William. Neither of them wanted to see him today, or ever again.

It really was a mess.

"We could tell her that she had to go on a long trip."

James offers.

"But then there's the 'where?' and 'when will she be back?'"

Jenny replies.

"She will still think she will get to see her at some point."

"Right enough."

He says, nodding.

"I know it won't be easy but – and tell me if it's absurd – we could just tell her the truth. I mean, a short version of it. Leave out the parts about her dad and stuff."

Jenny thinks for a moment.

"Just say she is a bad woman?"

James sighs.

"Yes. Unfortunately, that is the case, love."

They agree. This is what they will tell Dahlia and they will deal with any questions that come with that explanation.

"Will you be okay, love?"

He asks, stroking her hair.

"I could call Will and-"

"No. I still want Dahlia here."

She says, her tone strong.

"He's not winning this time."

James watches her as she stares out of the window, waiting to see her little girl run up the path.

He tries to let everything that has just happened, sink in. He tries to make sense of it but he can't. He remembers the time he saw those bruises on Jenny's body and how angry he was when he realised, that someone had did that to her; he was even more angry when he realised who.

Now, he can't believe her own mother was behind it all.

He conjures up a memory of his own mother; smiling and dancing while she was doing the dishes. He always loved that she danced, even when there was no music playing. He wonders if anyone ever hurt her, if her happiness was all a mask so that he and his siblings would never know the truth.

He lets his mind travel to the times when Jenny was most happy and he can't help but look at her now in admiration. She wore her smile, laughed her laugh and danced; even though she endured all of this hurt.

It dazzled him.

"You're beautiful, Jennifer."

He says, softly.

"You're the most beautiful woman in the world."

She turns to him and smiles.

"And you've travelled the world to know this?"

She asks.

"Don't need to."

He says, with such conviction.

"I could travel all the countries on the globe and I will never find a country, more beautiful and more homely; as the one that is your heart."

She blushes. He always knew just what to say to make her weak at the knees and she knows his words are exclusive to her only. No one else had ever heard him speak them. He didn't practice them before her, to pick up women in bars; he meant every word.

"You should get a job writing greeting cards."

She jokes.

"You'd turn nations to jelly."

They giggle, washing away all the seriousness.

"There's an idea, love."

She's about to sit beside him when she hears a car pulling up.

"The show must go on."

She says, plastering on a smile.

"Indeed."

He agrees.

"It must."

They open the door together and wait for Dahlia to run to them.

William doesn't get out of the car or look their way so there is no room for confrontation or dirty looks.

"Mommy!"

Dahlia runs up the path and into Jenny's arms. Jenny tries to lift her but finds herself too weak.

"Oh, you're getting such a big girl, sweetheart. I can't even lift you!"

James steps in and swoops her up with ease.

"Not too big for me, are ya, love? Let's fly."

He zooms her through the air, as he takes her to the living room and as Jenny is about to close the door, William catches her eye.

He looks sad, broken even and it occurs to Jenny that; her mother has gotten in touch with him.

Without thinking, she smiles wide, raises her hand as if to wave to him but instead; she flips him the bird and slams the door.

She had won this round.

"How was your day, sweetheart?"

She asks, as she enters the living room.

"Daddy made me pancakes and got my dolly a dress."

Dahlia's face lights up in excitement.

"And he got these!"

She pulls a pair of earrings from her little dungaree pocket.

"He said to give them to grandma."

Jenny's jaw drops as she recognises the earrings. They belong to her mother.

"Dahlia, sweetheart, when did daddy give you those?"

Dahlia puffs her cheeks out in concentration.

"We had to go back to get them because silly daddy forgot them."

She says, innocently; not aware of what this means.

"He said that it would rub salt in the woods."

Jenny clenches her jaw. She had just been flipped the bird back.

"What's wrong, love?"

James asks, when he notices the look on her face.

"Silly daddy is right, Dahlia."

Jenny says, ignoring James.

"He shouldn't have given you those."

She takes them from her and exits the room.

"Hey, love, you want to put your cartoons on?"

In Her Shadow

James asks Dahlia.

"Think your mummy has a headache and I'll need to find her some medicine."

Dahlia nods.

"Okay, I'll only be five minutes."

He switches the cartoons on and goes to find Jenny. He hears her angrily speaking to someone in the bedroom and gathers that, she must be on the phone.

He steps inside and she hangs up.

"I'll kill him, James!"

She throws the phone onto the bed.

"That's low. Even for him, that is low."

He still isn't sure what is going on and crosses to comfort her.

"What's happened, love?"

He asks.

"I'll stab him, James. I'll actually stab him."

He strokes her cheek.

"Calm down, love. Tell me-"

"Calm down? Calm down?"

She snaps.

"These, you know what they are?"

She shakes the earrings in his face.

"These are my mothers favourite earrings, don't you see?"

He doesn't.

"Do you- do you- do you want me to — to take them to her?"

He stutters.

She throws them to the ground and stomps on them.

"Listen to me, read my lips."

She says, slowly.

"They are her favourite earrings."

He gets it now.

"They're still-"
"Yes!"
James bites his lip.
"But, how-"
"I don't know, James! How does a sparrow fly?!"
He looks to his feet.
"Sorry, love."
Jenny sighs.
"I can do it, you know."
She says, her eyes wild.
"I can kill him. I can take a knife and-"
"Jennifer..."
James sits on the edge of the bed and buries his head in his hands.
"What?"
She snorts.
"What can they do to me, throw my coffin in a jail cell?"
James is about to reply, when Dahlia shuffles into the room.
"Mommy?"
She says.
Jenny looks to her in horror.
"Sweetheart, I-"
"Your mummy was just telling me about a movie she saw, love. The woman was very angry and upset but then it was all okay, in the end."
James takes her hand.
"Let's go finish your cartoons and let mummy rest."
He says, guiding her through the door..
"Jennifer, please think."
He tilts his head towards Dahlia.
"We'll be right in the living room."
Jenny throws herself onto the bed and tries to keep her

screaming internal. She puffs and she pants and tries to bring herself to a calm.

All she can see is red and all she can think about is William; paying for what he did – for what he is still doing –.

"James?"

She calls out.

"James, I need you in here."

James has just settled into the sofa with Dahlia and has her smiling but the sound of Jenny's voice, sends the coldest shiver down his spine. He must go to her.

"Dahlia, love."

He says, voice unsteady.

"I forgot to get your mummy the medicine. I'll be back in a little moment, okay?"

She nods up at him.

"Okay, daddy."

She says, catching him off guard.

"James, love."

He says, correcting her.

"You said-"

"I know."

She cuts in, excited.

"I've decided, I have two daddies. Alexander in my class has two daddies. You're daddy two and daddy is daddy one."

She smiles.

James ruffles her hair. He can't think of how to respond and before he lets himself get overwhelmed with emotion, he goes to Jenny.

"Love?"

He whispers, as he enters the room.

"Where are you?"

As he steps further inside, he finds her; squeezed into the space between their wardrobe and the wall.

He kneels in front of her.
"I can't do it."
She says, her face drained of all colour.
"I just can't."
He nods.
"Of course, love. That's not the answer."
He says, thinking she's still talking about killing William.
"Not that!"
She snaps.
"I don't care about him. I wouldn't waste my time."
He rests his hands on her knees.
"Then, what can't you do, love? I'll help you."
She places her hands on his. They are cold and wet from her tears.
"I can't die."
She whispers.
"It's not my time. It's not fair."
He squeezes her knees and bites his lip. This isn't something that he can help her with – keep her alive – but he will remain closer than close to her, while she is still here.
"I know, love."
He says, his body trembling.
"I know."
He gives her that 'sad puppy' look and she squeezes his hands.
"We have to prepare her, James. It can't just end."
Tears spill from his eyes and onto her hands; mixing with her tears.
"How?"
He croaks out.
"How can we just-"
"Together."
Jenny answers.

In Her Shadow

"Like we do everything else."

Chapter 18: That's What Makes The Stars Shine

Jenny and James compose themselves and return to Dahlia; who sits – intently – watching her cartoons.

They sit either side of her.

"Dahlia…"

Jenny starts.

"Do you mind if we switch this off for a little minute? We need to talk to you about something."

James bites down on his lip, harder than usual and tries to suppress any tears; that threaten to fall.

Dahlia nods.

"I watched this one already anyway, mommy."

Jenny smiles.

"I think I remember that one too." She says, knowing she has definitely watched it over 50 times, or more.

"Is it about daddy two?"

Dahlia asks.

"Alexander said he has two daddies and they love him very much and I told him, I have two daddies too. Was that bad?"

Jenny touches her hand to Dahlia's cheek.

"No, sweetheart…"

She says, touched that she sees James as a father figure.

"No, that wasn't bad. We want to talk to you about me – mommy –."

"Alexander doesn't have a mommy."

In Her Shadow

Dahlia says.

"He said some people have two daddies and other people have two mommies. Is that true, mommy? Do some people get two mommies?"

Jenny nods.

"Yes, some people get two mommies."

She smiles.

"But this is about your mommy."

"You will only ever have one mummy, Dahlia."

James adds.

"And sometimes mummies..."

He can't continue.

Jenny takes a deep breath.

"Sometimes mommies... have to go away."

Her voice starts to shake.

"But it doesn't mean that they stop loving you."

She finishes.

Dahlia looks up at her confused.

"Where do they go?"

She asks.

James looks to Jenny and nods. He's ready to continue.

"Well, it's like my mummy, love... she went to the stars, remember?"

Dahlia nods.

"And you know; the stars are very, very far away so it's not easy to – to just come back."

Jenny clears her throat.

"James' mom is up there on her own, sweetheart and mommy was thinking-"

"We can all go and visit her?"

Dahlia asks.

Jenny and James sniff back some tears.

"No, sweetheart. Just me. Only one person can go at a

time."

Dahlia's eyes start to fill up.

"But that means you can't come back."

She says.

"I'll never see you again."

Jenny lets her tears spill.

"Thing is, love."

James wipes his face.

"Just because you won't see her, doesn't mean she's not there."

He sniffs.

"You know the brightest star, the one I always point to?"

She nods.

"That's my mummy's star. That's where your mummy will be going and-"

"I don't want mommy to go."

She cries.

James bites down on his lip once more and Jenny breathes in, then out, then in, then out again.

"I don't want to go either, sweetheart."

She says, finally.

"It's just-"

"Did God tell you to go?"

This question takes Jenny by surprise. She had never spoken to Dahlia about religion as she wanted her to grow up; without feeling the pressure that someone may be watching her every move, from a distance. That's the way Jenny grew up and James wasn't religious at all so, she didn't learn of God in their home.

"No. No, Dahlia."

She says.

"This is just-"

"It's just something that happens sometimes."

In Her Shadow

James cuts in.

"Some people have to go to the stars... It's what keeps them shining."

He says, trying to make it sound magical for her.

Dahlia stops crying.

"So it's mommy's new job?"

She asks.

They take a deep breath and nod.

"And James will stay here and look after the diner for me."

Jenny says, going with James' theory about; what makes the stars shine.

"Can I look after it too?"

Dahlia asks.

Again, James and Jenny nod.

They don't have the energy to explain that, that might not happen. William might not let her see James again – in spite of what he said to James previously –. They were taking this one step at a time.

"Do I still get to be a princess?"

They smile at Dahlia's question. Her innocence and inability to understand death touches them and they both wish that everyone could stay this innocent forever.

Forever – they thought – would be the most wonderful gift.

"Of course, love."

James replies, latching onto that happy thought.

"Not letting your mum wriggle out of marrying me."

Jenny smiles.

"I wouldn't even try."

They all sit in a comfortable silence for a few moments, letting the previous conversation sink in; before they dust themselves off and carry on.

"Can we watch the cartoons again?"

Says Dahlia, breaking the silence.

"Sure, sweetheart."
Jenny replies.
"But, there's something else."
"There is?"
James asks.
"Yeah, your grandmother can't-"
"I know."
Says Dahlia.
"Daddy said that grandma June couldn't make it."
James clenches his jaw.
"No, sweetheart. She couldn't, not today."
Says Jenny, trying not to worry about what William has actually told her."
"We will still have a good time though."
James says, perking up a little.
"In fact, I've just thought of a game we could play." Dahlia jumps up in excitement and Jenny looks at him, wondering where this is going.
"What's it called?"
Dahlia asks.
"It's called…"
James says, with a grin.
"Tickle yourself silly."
Jenny laughs.
"What?"
"Tickle yourself silly, love. It's where you tickle yourself, just like this."
He stars tickling himself.
"And first to laugh wins."
Jenny rolls her eyes.
"You can't tickle yourself, it doesn't work."
He sighs.
"Well, duh!"

In Her Shadow

He says.

"That's why the first to laugh is the winner. If you manage to actually tickle yourself, you've won the game."

Jenny shakes her head.

"So we sit here all night until-"

"Look, mommy! I can tickle myself and be a gorilla at the same time."

Dahlia starts making monkey noises and James and Jenny burst into a fit of giggles.

"Aw, you win, Dahlia."

James says, his heart filling; with the warmest love.

"Hey! I thought the first to laugh was the winner?"

Jenny says, shoving him.

"I got it mixed up, love. It was the first to provide the laugh who wins. Yeah, that's it."

They all laugh together now, like they had no worries and no cares.

They were as pretty as a postcard once more. One that would read, 'don't you wish you were here?'

They were happy. Genuinely.

Chapter 19: The 'Thank You'

It's a Friday night – the night before Jenny and James are to be married – and they're sitting at their kitchen table, sipping on coffee.

Jenny takes a deep breath and sighs.

"Do you think it was the right thing to do?"

She asks.

"What's that, love?"

James replies.

"Asking my dad to pick Dahlia up from William's tomorrow."

"Would you want him dropping her off here though? I mean, neither of us want to see him and more especially, on our wedding day."

Jenny huffs.

"She should be here tonight anyway."

James shrugs.

"I know, love. She doesn't understand though. She wants her dad to see her in her dress and she wants him to be the one to braid her hair."

"I know. I just feel really sorry for my dad."

She says, not liking that he was her only option; in who would pick Dahlia up.

"Me too, love."

James seconds.

"Did you tell him?"

Jenny shakes her head.

"How do you even start that conversation?"

She asks, really not knowing.

"I don't know."
He sighs.
"He does know that you don't what your mother there though, yeah?"
Jenny nods.
"He didn't even ask why."
She says, shrugging her shoulders.
"So, you didn't have an opening to tell him."
He says, trying to make her feel better.
"With things like that, love, you know anyway."
She narrows her eyes at him.
"You think he knows?"
She asks, not quite sure.
"He knew before, didn't he?"
She nods.
"Then, he'll know now."
James says, stretching his hand out for her to take it. She does.
"All we can do is be there for him, love."
He says, letting her know that; he was behind her and on her dad's side too.
Jenny nods again and drops her eyes to their hands.
"Does it feel right?"
She asks, shifting the subject.
"Marrying me tomorrow, does it feel right?"
He squeezes her hand.
"Why would it feel otherwise?"
Jenny slowly raises her head and looks him in the eye.
"You know when they say 'the old ball and chain?'"
James nods.
"Yeah, what of that, love?"
She grazes his cheek with her free hand.
"I don't want to be your ball and chain, James."

She says, seriously.

"When I go down..."

She continues, referring to when they lower her coffin.

"I don't want to pull you down there with me."

James goes to speak but she hasn't finished.

"Listen."

She says, touching her fingertips to his lips.

"When you stand up here tomorrow and you promise – in front of our guests – that you will love me in sickness and in health and till death do us part; I want you to think about that last line. I want you to mean it."

James kisses her fingertips.

"Of course."

He says, taking hold of both of her hands now.

"I haven't left your side from day we met, love."

She shakes her head.

"Till death."

She says slowly.

"Do us part. We part when I go, you understand?"

He doesn't.

"Love, I don't know what you want me to say here. I'm sorry."

She takes a deep breath.

"When I go, I go for good. You live on."

She says.

"I'm not your ball and chain."

It's sinking in. She's telling him that death is the end, that his vows are no longer valid when it occurs and he can move on without her. He doesn't like this.

"Till death do us part."

He looks her in the eye.

"Not till my death do us part, not till your death do us part. 'Till death'."

He leans closer to her.

"My heart will only love you, until it stops beating and then; I will make my way to the afterlife and whatever bloody heaven you have built your home in and I will come knocking on that door, and beg you take me in." He says, getting emotional.

"You're it for me, Jennifer."

He sniffs.

"There's no one who walks this earth; who could tread as beautifully as you did, into my life. No one."

Jenny sinks back into her seat. She had never seen so much passion exude from one being before. He filled the room with his words, wrapped them around her and made sure that she could feel them; right in the very core of her. He was 'it' for her too.

"Then, I will let you in."

She says, accepting that; he won't let her go.

"I will wait for you."

James bites down on his lip and Jenny blows her fringe from her eyes.

"I didn't mean to make it cold."

She says, meaning the atmosphere.

James smiles.

"You never make it cold, love. You always keep me warm."

They both sigh and shake their heads.

"I'm telling you, you're wasted in that diner."

She giggles.

"Greeting cards are your calling."

She jokes.

"So I can turn nations into a wobbly dessert?"

They both laugh.

In all the time they had been together, they hadn't had many 'too serious' moments. They always manage to laugh everything off but even now, as they laugh; their hearts are breaking.

They're the only ones who can see through each others masks though; so they know this but, they don't touch it. They keep gifting smiles to each other.

"So, Dahlia's dress will be blue?"

Jenny asks, wanting to take their minds off of the 'till death' moment.

"I think so, love. I don't know if he returned the purple one though."

"Purple?"

"Oh, that's right! I didn't tell you."

He says, shaking his head.

"Will thought her favourite colour was purple."

Jenny rolls her eyes.

"Typical."

She says.

"I know."

He agrees.

"But hey, you're both going to look beautiful no matter what colour you're wearing."

"Well, you know I'm wearing black."

"You know what I mean. You'll both be beautiful."

Jenny smiles.

"And you?"

She asks.

"I'm wearing the white, love."

He replies.

"Duh!"

She tuts.

"I mean, how will you look?"

James laughs.

"Well... like me. Only, I'll be wearing white."

Jenny sighs.
"You'll be beautiful too."
She says.
She wished just once that; James would have something nice to say about himself, as well as about her.
"I was hoping to hear you compliment yourself, at least once before-"
"Before we are married."
James interrupts. Not wanting her to say, before she dies.
"Yes."
She nods.
"Before we are married."
He smiles.
"Well, I do, love."
He says.
"The most beautiful thing about me is you and I compliment you."
She rolls her eyes again.
"You're hard work, James Baker."
He laughs.
"I do apologise, Mrs Baker."
She shoves him lightly.
"Don't jinx it!"
He sighs.
"Aw, love, I'm too excited. Can't you let me away with that one?"
She smiles.
"I suppose.
She says.
"But just that one."
"Deal."
He nods.
"You know what?"

He scratches his head and sighs.
"What?"
She asks.
"These coffees will be as cold as a polar bear's arse."
He replies.
"Should I make us another?"
Jenny bursts out laughing.
"Yeah, maybe just stick with the diner after all, baby. I don't think we'll ever see that one on a birthday card."
He smirks.
"I don't know, love, 'Happy Birthday' is a bit overdone, don't you think?"
"Ah well, there's hope for you yet."
She smiles.
"Go on, then. Can never have too much blood in your caffeine."
She says.
"Too much caff-"
"I said what I said."
James rolls his eyes.
"I'll get right on it, love."
Jenny watches him as he waits for the kettle to boil. He can feel her eyes on him but he doesn't turn around.
They enjoy the silence as it visits momentarily and try to think of something else to talk about, over their second coffee.
James prepares the mugs and Jenny continues to watch. She's always loved the way he moves; his body language never threatening and each little gesture, more endearing than the last. She used to joke to herself that she dreamed him, that he wasn't really real and that he was just a figment of her imagination.
She loved romance books, movies and sad songs; the kind

of songs that try to win a lover back. She didn't believe someone like James existed beyond those pages, those tear-jerking scenes and soft melodies but there he was; standing right in front of her and he was all hers. Every little part of him, belonged to her.

She feels guilty. She had taken everything he had – everything he had given her – and he didn't want it back. Even though, she wouldn't be around much longer to repay him.

"There we are."
He places her cup in front of her and sits back down.
"I don't have a penny on me, love but it would nice to know what's on your mind."
He waves his hand in front of her face.
"Where have you gone?"
She snaps out of her thoughts.
"Nowhere, I'm right here. I was just thinking about the diner."
She says, not completely lying.
"Right."
He replies.
"Something need doing?"
She shakes her head.
"No, I was just thinking how I never really thanked you for it."
"You thanked me."
He says, taking a sip of his coffee.
"I know I said 'thank you' but I don't think you know, just how much it meant – it means to me -.
She says, trying to find the right words.
"I know, love."
She shakes her head.
"No. No, you don't."
This time, she stretches her arm across the table for him to

take her hand. He does.

"That was my dream as a child. I watched 'Grease' and I wanted a diner, just like that."

She sighs.

"As I grew older and after I had Dahlia, I gave up on that dream. I didn't believe in it anymore but when I met you, you not only restored my belief; you believed too."

James shakes his head.

"What are you doing?"

He asks.

She didn't have to do this. He was very much aware of what the diner meant to her and he knew; how much she valued him also. He didn't need reassuring.

"I'm thanking you."

She replies.

"Love-"

"No, let me do this."

She pleads.

"I need you to know that I haven't taken anything – I haven't taken you – for granted.

James – although he knows what he means to her – lets her continue. She needed to get it all off her chest.

"I wish it were you."

She starts.

"I wished on every star, to turn back time and make it you."

James nods. He knows what she means, as he had the same wish. Dahlia wasn't his daughter and he will never get to have his own child with Jenny and so, he wished it was him also. He wished he met her sooner.

"That little girl has magic in her eyes. She didn't get that from me or him, James."

She smiles.

"You are the one who brought the magic."

In Her Shadow

He shakes his head.

"No, love. She got those eyes from you."

Jenny laughs.

"No, baby. You remember when I asked you about heaven?"

He nods slowly, not really wanting to delve into the 'do you believe?' conversation again.

"I only believe there is a heaven because of you."

She says, squeezing his hand.

"I grew up being told that God and angels and Adam and Eve were all real, that they walked – and maybe still walk – this earth and I never believed it."

She swallows the lump in her throat.

"At least now I can leave knowing that; angels do walk the earth but, they aren't how they describe them to you in Sunday school."

She smiles wide.

"You didn't come with wings, James but you always helped me fly and you might not have a halo or a harp but, you have the most seraphic heart and your words are more beautiful, more affirming than anything; written down, in any bible – owned by any man or woman, of any religion."

She touches her hand to his cheek and wipes away the tears that fall.

"You're my angel."

She whispers.

"It doesn't hurt anymore."

James stands – making the chair legs screech – and pulls her up and into his arms.

He squeezes her tighter than he means to but he doesn't let go.

"And you're my religion, love."

He sobs.

In Her Shadow

"I'll never stop believing in you."

They stand, holding each other for what feels like an eternity. They have nothing more to say and when they manage to tear themselves away from each other; they retire to bed and rest.

Tomorrow is their special day and they couldn't wait to get to it.

In Her Shadow

Chapter 20: It Looks Better On

"Wakey wakey, eggs and bakey…"
Jenny has her singsong voice on and James opens his eyes and smiles from ear to ear, as he takes in her beautiful, sleepy look.
"Morning, love."
He stretches.
"I don't smell that bacon you're singing about."
He sniffs the air.
"Or the eggs. You're gonna have to find a better way to get me out of this bed."
Jenny rolls her eyes.
"Your sister will be here soon."
She says.
"Nope, the bed is too comfy."
He laughs.
"Third time lucky, love?"
Jenny purses her lips.
"Well, There's this thing on today."
She smiles.
"I don't know if you will be up for it but I hear it's going to be nice."
James grins.
"Yeah? What's that, love?"
"You want me to say it, don't you?"
She huffs.
"Wouldn't hurt, love."
He replies.
"It's our wedding day."

She says, throwing up her hands in a 'TA-DA' motion.
James bites his lip.
"That'll do it, love."
He says, stretching once more.
"I'll definitely get up for that."
Jenny leans in and kisses him and before he even gets the chance to run his fingers through her hair, the doorbell rings.
"That'll be Kate."
He sighs.
"It's like she just knows."
Kate Is James' sister. She is his only sibling who will make it to their wedding as, she is the only one who lives in New York. The others, stayed put in London.
"I'll get it."
Jenny decides.
"I'm dying to see her."
She screws her face up at her choice of words.
"I didn't-"
"I'll come with you, love."
James pulls on some pyjama bottoms and heads to answer the door with her.
"Kate!"
Jenny wraps her arms around her and pulls her inside.
"We are so happy you could make it."
She says, her voice high pitched.
James stands back.
"Can the little brother get a hug as well, please?"
He says, holding his arms out.
"Can the big sister get through the door first, please?"
Laughs Kate.
Jenny lets her go.
"Sorry, I'm just so excited."
James pulls his sister in for a big cuddle and Jenny beams

with admiration as she watches them.

"You look stunning, Kate. I love that dress."

James lets her go and she smiles at Jenny.

"I picked it up in a sale. It's not the one I'm wearing to the wedding."

Jenny takes her hand and leads her to the living room.

"I knew you were hiding something in that case. Show me, show me."

She claps her hands as they sit on the sofa.

"I think it's a bit plain, Jenny but I don't know." James sits in the armchair across from them.

"I'm sure it'll be lovely, sis."

He says, smiling at them both.

They look at him with raised eyebrows.

"What?"

He asks.

"You're actually going to sit and talk dresses with us?"

Kate asks.

"Why not?"

He shrugs.

"Because, you have to go and get yourself sorted."

Jenny says, flicking her eyes to the clock on the wall.

"My dad will be here soon and you can both swap fashion tips."

James laughs.

"Don't think any of us know much about fashion, love but, I will leave you to it."

He plants a kiss on Jenny's forehead and squeezes Kate's shoulder, before exiting the room.

Kate leans in to Jenny.

"So..."

She says.

"Do I get to see the dress?"

Jenny smiles.
"I should think so. You'll have to help me into it."
They laugh.
"About your dad…"
Kate wonders.
"He likes James?"
Jenny nods.
"They haven't known each other long but I know he does."
Kate smiles.
"They've never liked him, you know. Girls dads. But he has a heart of gold."
Jenny half smiles.
James had never spoken about the girls that had come before her so this remark threw her a little.
"I know."
She says, agreeing.
"He's the best."
Kate senses she has put her foot in it.
"There weren't many."
She says, quickly.
"And they didn't last long."
Jenny shrugs.
"I didn't think he was a monk, until he met me."
She says, looking down.
"It's just an odd conversation, is all."
Kate nods.
"So, we drop it. I'm sorry."
She says.
"So, you're wearing black?"
Jenny accepts this subject change.
"Yeah and James will be wearing white."
Kate smiles.
"That'll be a nice change."

In Her Shadow

She says, nudging Jenny's knee.
"I don't really get his whole black phase."
Jenny shifts slightly.
"That's my fault."
She whispers, hoping Kate will leave this subject alone also.
"Not a fault, love. It's a pleasure."
James interrupts, taking a seat in the armchair again.
"Your dad is on his way, love. Okay if I wait for him here?"
Jenny nods.
"Of course. We have plenty of time."
Kate is confused.
"What do you mean, it's your fault he wears only black?"
James motions to her to drop it but she doesn't notice.
"Well..."
Jenny starts.
"Love, you don't-"
"No, James, It's okay."
It's not okay but she figures; it's best to get it over with, otherwise Kate will just ask more and more questions.
James sighs.
"I'm her shadow, Kate, okay? I-"
"Her shadow?"
Kate's confusion deepens.
"I was married before."
Confesses Jenny.
"He was – he wasn't very nice."
"How so?"
Kate asks, not really knowing how far is too far to push; when it comes to wanting to know more.
"Kate... Just drop it."
James says, scowling at her.
Kate really doesn't get it. To anyone else - being told to 'drop it' would be enough indication that; this topic, isn't a

pleasant topic. But not to Kate. She turns to Jenny and looks at her expectantly, willing her to continue.

James is about to intervene once more but Jenny holds her hand up.

"James, It's okay. I want to explain."

He sits back and leaves her to continue.

"He was violent. With his words and his actions."

Kate gets it now. This really was none of her business and she is sorry she asked and she looks to James, who gives her a 'too late now' look."

"I'm so sorry, Jenny I-"

"It's okay."

Jenny smiles at them both.

"While I was with him, I wore a lot of black myself."

She shrugs.

"I thought it would somehow make me more invisible, like I wasn't there, you know?"

Kate nods.

"When I left him and I met your brother; I hadn't quite shaken off that feeling of wanting to be invisible so, I continued wearing the black."

She sighs.

"Then on our third date, James gifted me the most beautiful, most colourful dress and I was so overwhelmed. I cried."

James leans forward and takes her hand.

"So, I asked her why it made her so sad."

He says.

"And I told him about the wanting to be invisible but I never told him about the abuse."

Jenny continues.

"So, on our next date, I wore the dress."

"And I showed up in black."

James adds.

"And he asked if it would be okay if he wore the black from then on, while I showed all of my colours to the world."

James laughs.

"I think she thought I was a bit mad but by the eighth date, I had convinced her to shine.

Didn't I, love?"

He says, squeezing her hand.

Kate frowns.

"Why couldn't you both wear colours?"

She asks.

James laughs again.

"Wouldn't look much like a shadow then, would I?"

Kate still doesn't understand and she is over the line now so doesn't see the harm in stepping further.

"Jenny, I don't get it."

Jenny smiles.

"At a time when I was frightened of my own shadow?"

She nods towards James.

"He wanted me to see that not all shadows are to be feared."

She says.

"But..."

Kate says.

"He didn't know about the abuse."

James nods his head.

"Some things you just know, Kate."

Before she can ask anymore questions, there is a knock on the door.

"That'll be your dad, love. I'll get it."

Kate gives herself a shake.

"What do I call him?"

She asks, nervously.

"Who?"
Jenny replies.
"Your dad."
"Oh! His name."
"I don't his name, Jenny."
Kate whisper's as Richard enters the room with James.
"Are you getting married in those pyjamas, Jenny?"
Jenny laughs.
"Obviously not, dad."
She says, hugging him.
"Then, why on earth are you still in them? It's your wedding day!"
"That's how you do it, love."
James chuckles, referring to their earlier conversation.
"Richard, this is my sister Kate."
Richard shakes her hand and throws a glance to James.
"Your all cheekbones, your family. Look at this one! She could be a model."
Kate blushes.
"Her head is big enough, Richard."
Says James, jokingly.
"All cheekbones and foreheads, us lot. Eh, Kate?"
She shoves him.
"Speak for yourself. Could write the bible on that forehead!"
Richard laughs.
"And you used to want a brother or sister."
He says to Jenny.
Jenny smiles.
"As much as I'm enjoying this little back and forth..."
She turns to James.
"It's our wedding day."
James rolls his eyes.

"Right, that's us told, Richard. Better let the girls get their glam on."

Jenny laughs.

"Did you learn that phrase from a fashion magazine?"

She asks, thinking that's where phrases like that; would usually be found.

"Doctor's waiting room, love. They're full of them."

He bites his lip. He didn't mean to bring the doctors up but he couldn't take it back.

"Right, Richard... time to go and pamper ourselves pretty."

Jenny laughs again.

"Have fun!"

They leave the girls in the living room and go to the bedroom.

James starts picking clothes up off of the floor and Richard struggles with something in his pocket.

He pulls out a box.

"Here, son."

He says, thrusting it towards him.

James turns around.

"What's this?"

"A gift."

He takes the box from Richard and opens it slowly. Inside, there is a watch.

"I don't have any cufflinks, otherwise you would've gotten those."

James shakes his head.

"Richard, I can't-"

"You will."

"But-"

Richard throws his hands up.

"Son, if you don't take it, I'll be very offended."

James nods.

"Thank you. Thank you very-"

"Here, the strap is tricky. I'll put it on for you."

Richard takes the box and proceeds to put the watch around James' wrist.

"It doesn't come with a story, I'm afraid."

He says, shaking his head.

"It's new. We don't do heirlooms and sentiment at our home."

James smiles.

"The greatest gift I've ever received is your daughter, Richard."

He says, his knees knocking together.

"Our home was full of trinkets and memories but nothing ever meant so much to me as your daughter does."

Richard nods.

"I know you mean that, son."

He shakes James' hand firmly and makes sure the watch can be seen.

"Suits you."

He says, nodding his head.

In the living room, Jenny is running her fingers through her hair and giving Kate an 'I give up' look.

"I don't know, Kate. I didn't really think about that part."

Kate tuts.

"You must've seen some style you liked somewhere. You can't just walk down the aisle with it, hanging like curtains."

She teases.

"What about a bun?"

Jenny asks.

"What kind of bun?"

Kate replies.

"Just the usual kind."

Says Jenny, not knowing there's more than one way to do a

bun.

"Are you bonkers? You seriously want to get married, looking like you're doing the hoovering?"

Jenny shakes her head.

"Well, no. obviously but, I really don't have a clue, Kate."

"I'll curl it."

Kate says.

"You have a curling iron, right?"

Jenny shakes her head.

"Bloody hell, Jenny! Please tell me you at least have a pair of straighteners?"

"Oh! Those I do have."

She replies, nodding her head.

"Then I'll curl it with them."

Kate says.

Jenny looks at her confused.

"How can you curl my hair with them, when they're supposed to straighten your hair?"

"Honestly, Jenny... It's like you just became a girl yesterday."

Jenny laughs nervously. She never really had any friends and she didn't have a good relationship with her mother so, she never got to do the girly thing. She didn't pamper herself or read fashion magazines.

"James paints my nails sometimes."

She says, holding her hands up.

"If we are going out somewhere.... James paints them for me. I don't really know how to do those things so I ask him to."

Kate snorts.

"And he knows how?"

"His hand is more steady than mine."

Jenny replies, dropping her hands.

"Yeah but, come on, Jenny. James is not the most

effeminate of men."

"He's not a brute either, Kate."

Kate laughs.

"Maybe not the James you know but he had his fair share of fights, back in the day."

"Fights, that he didn't start."

Jenny replies, defending him. She knew of James' past and how he was bullied and how he stood up for himself, in the end. This didn't make him any less of a gentle person. He did what he had to do.

"Oh, but he knew how to finish them."

Kate says, almost catty.

"You know what, I think I'll just straighten my hair."

Says Jenny, not wanting Kate to touch her hair.

"That's more me."

Kate shrugs.

"Suit yourself. I was only trying to help."

Suddenly, Kate didn't seem so friendly to Jenny. She had only met her a handful of times before and hadn't spent enough time in her company, to know her well. She didn't like how she was coming across now. It was almost as if, she was trying to turn Jenny against James.

"I'll be right back."

She says, heading to the bedroom and leaving Kate on the sofa.

"Jennifer, love, you okay?"

She enters the room.

"Yeah... I was just wondering if it would be okay to steal you for five minutes?"

Richard smiles.

"I'll just pop in and keep..."

He searches for her name.

"Kate."

In Her Shadow

Says Jenny.
"I'll keep Kate company."
He says, leaving them both alone.
Jenny sits on the edge of the bed and James follows.
"What's up, love?"
She shakes her head.
"Nothing."
She lies.
"I just wanted to be with you."
He nods.
"It's strange having them here, isn't it? Too used to it being just us and Dahlia sometimes, eh?"
She smiles.
"I guess."
James strokes her hair.
"Kate gonna do your hair for ya, love?"
She shakes her head.
"I'm going to straighten it."
He runs his fingers gently through the ends.
"More you."
He replies, as if he read her mind.
Jenny clears her throat.
"Does Kate know?"
She asks, timidly.
"Know what, love?"
"About me. That I'm... you know."
James hangs his head.
"I let you down, love, didn't I? I said you could tell me anything and I wouldn't tell anyone but-"
"But it's a heavy thing to carry on your own."
She says, understanding.
"No matter how strong you are."
He sighs.

"I'm not strong, Jennifer. Sometimes I find it hard to put my feet to the floor and stand but then you smile or you laugh and I borrow some strength from you."

She leans against him.

"You're stronger than you think, James."

He shakes his head.

"Did she bring it up? She shouldn't-"
"No. No, she didn't. I could just tell."

James clenches his jaw.

"Do you want me to say something?"

She shakes her head.

"No."

He pulls her into him and drops a gentle kiss onto her shoulder.

"Are you happy?"

He asks, looking up at her.

Jenny pulls away, takes his face in her hands and stares, deep into his eyes.

"The happiest I'll ever be."

She says.

He smiles and they share a kiss, before Jenny heads back to the living room.

"Right, dad. I'm going to get into my dress now so you have to keep James in the room."

"Got it."

He says, giving her a 'thumbs up'.

"Nice chatting with you, Kate."

He leaves.

"Everything okay?"

Kate asks, more worrying about what Jenny was telling James; rather than her well-being.

"Everything is perfect."

Jenny replies.

"It's my wedding day."

Kate smiles.

"Your dad was telling me he's going to pick your daughter up soon."

Jenny smiles back.

"Yeah, she's so excited."

Kate drops her head.

"I can imagine."

She says, scuffling her feet on the carpet.

Jenny detects that there is something Kate isn't saying but she doesn't ask her what. She didn't want any drama today.

"So, will you help me get my dress on?"

She asks.

"I had a shower this morning and I was so tempted to put it on afterwards but, well, it would be bad luck, right?"

Kate nods.

"I'll help you."

Jenny disappears and returns with her dress. She managed to keep it hidden from James and as she carries it now, she wonders how that was even possible. It was very puffy.

"It seemed much smaller in the shop."

She laughs.

"Most things do, until they're in a confined space." Kate replies.

Jenny ignores this. She thinks Kate was having a dig at their small apartment and isn't in the mood to explain to her that, this was home. This was the only place they could afford and they loved it.

"True."

She says.

"But it is a big dress."

"Indeed."

Kate says.

In Her Shadow

"Right then. We better get cracking."

She takes the dress from Jenny and tries to find something she likes about it but she can't. It was just too over the top for her liking.

"What made you decide on this one anyway, Jenny?"

She asks, her nose turned up.

"It looks a lot better when it's on, Kate." Jenny says, stripping down to her underwear.

"Do you think I should step into it or will you manage to slide it over my head?"

She asks.

Kate is about to reply but is left speechless when she looks at her and takes in her fragile and pale frame.

"It's winter."

Jenny says, nervously.

"A bit hard to be a radiant, sun-kissed bride."

Kate shakes her head.

"Yeah, it's- it's cold."

She says.

She sets the dress down on the sofa.

"Jenny, I can't do it."

Jenny gazes at her, unsure of what she can't do.

"Best to step into it?"

Kate runs her hands through her hair and sighs.

"I just don't want to – I don't want to... I can't."

She goes to leave the room but Jenny stands in her way.

"You can't what? You can't even pretend to be happy for us?"

She hisses.

"Jenny, get out of the way."

Kate warns.

"You need to get out of my way."

Jenny doesn't budge.

In Her Shadow

"What are you doing, Kate? Can't you just-"

"No, I can't. You don't understand."

Jenny shrugs.

"Try me. Tell me what I don't understand."

Kate folds her arms in defiance.

"If you don't move out of the way, I will call James in here."

Jenny smiles.

"I'll call him for you, if you like."

Kate sneers.

"How can you do this to him? How can you just do this?"

"Do what?"

Jenny whispers.

"You're pulling him along, like your little puppet and then you're gonna cut the strings and leave him on the shelf."

She says, hitting hard.

"How can you do that?"

Jenny's jaw drops.

"I don't have a choice."

She says, angered.

"Do you think I want to die, Kate?"

"Yeah, well our mum didn't either, Jenny."

Jenny leans against the door as all the energy she had, escapes from her body.

"This is about your mom?"

She asks, feeling ashamed that she didn't even stop to think, what this must be doing to Kate.

"That's why you can't-"

"She looked just like that."

She points a shaking finger towards Jenny's bare flesh.

"All drawn in and bones sticking out."

She sniffs.

"He's lost too much."

Jenny reaches out to give her a hug but she shakes away.
"Don't touch me."
She snaps.
"I'm sorry, Kate."
"Not that sorry."
Kate replies.
"You're still going to drag him up that aisle, aren't you?"
Jenny shakes her head.
"He wants this, Kate. I-"
"But he doesn't need it."
She cuts in.

Jenny opens the door and let's Kate leave. She closes it behind her and takes a seat in the armchair.

She is about to get up and put the dress on herself when a knock on the living room door interrupts her.

"You decent, love?"
James calls through.
"The dress is on the sofa."
She calls back.
"And you are?"
"Sitting in the armchair."
He slowly opens the door.
"I promise I won't look to the sofa, love."
He closes the door and kneels in front of her.
"I heard the bathroom door slam and thought I'd come and see if everything was okay. Is it?"
He asks, searching for the answer in her eyes.
She shakes her head.
"Kate doesn't like my dress."
She says, not wanting to get into it.
"Oh, right."
He says, surprised.
"Good thing she's not the one wearing it then, isn't it?"

In Her Shadow

She nods.

He tries to break into her thoughts and see what else is troubling her but as always, she was good at hiding them.

"She only slams doors when she's in a mood or upset, love."

He says, trying to get more out of her.

"Do you want to talk about it?"

Jenny grips onto the sides of the chair.

"I love you so much, James. I want to marry you more than anything but-"

"I won't hear a 'but', love."

He says, cutting her off.

"Especially if chatting to Kate has brought it about."

She sighs.

"She just really cares about you, baby."

"Right. Then, there's no problem."

He shrugs.

"If she cares about me – as much as you think she does – then, there's no problem here."

Jenny strokes his face.

"Your mom..."

She starts.

"What would she have said to me?"

James rests his head in Jenny's lap and sighs. He wasn't expecting such a question.

"She probably would have told you you're too young to get married, to be honest."

He smiles.

"But, she would've given her blessing anyway, love."

Jenny runs her fingertips through his hair.

"Even when-"

"Even then, love."

He strokes her tummy and tilts his head to look up at her.

"She wouldn't even bring it up."

He says, reassuring her.

"She didn't when she was the one wearing those shoes, Jennifer so yes, even then."

Jenny nods.

She knew that his mother never told him – or any of her children – that she was sick and she couldn't help but wonder if James – knowing that Jenny was – would make it easier for him; when she was gone. They always say, it's the not knowing that's the worst and so Jenny would like to think that him knowing, means it won't be as difficult to deal with. She knows deep down though, that it'll hit him just as hard as his mother's death.

She gives herself a shake.

"Then, there's no problem."

She says, smiling.

"Dad should go and get Dahlia soon. She will be bursting with excitement."

James doesn't move. He enjoys the comfort of her lap a little longer and Jenny doesn't mind. She felt far too weak to stand at the moment anyway.

"Plenty of time."

He says, closing his eyes.

"Plenty of time.

She repeats.

In Her Shadow

Chapter 21: Nothing Good About 'Goodbye'

James and Kate are sitting in the bedroom.
He will have to leave very soon as Dahlia is on her way with Richard, to get Jenny and take her to the hall; they have booked for the wedding.
He wants to make sure everything has settled first though.
"How's the dress looking?"
He asks.
"It's nice."
Kate replies.
"Jenny said you didn't like it and that's why you stormed off."
Kate hangs her head.
"I was just having one of my moments."
She says, not wanting to talk about the conversation; she had with Jenny.
"You know what I'm like."
He nods.
"Everything is okay now though, yeah?"
Kate smiles.
"I went back in didn't I?"
James smirks.
"Not what I asked, Kate."
She shakes her head.
"What more do you want from me, James?"
She asks, deflated.

"I went back, I fixed her hair, I helped her on with her dress and now I'm here; letting her have a moment to collect herself."

He sighs.

"Just want you to understand that, I need this."

He says, looking her in the eye.

"She's it for me."

Kate rolls her eyes.

"James, you're only 38. There will be-"

"No there won't. There won't be anyone else, Kate."

He stands.

"I know you don't get it, sis. But I know my own heart and I gave it to Jennifer, on day one. I won't be taking it back to give to some shoddy imitation of her, through time."

She stands beside him, accepting that there is nothing she can say to change his mind and she lets it drop.

"Then, we better get you out of here so you can marry her, eh?"

She says, with all the phony enthusiasm she could muster.

James nods.

"I want to say goodbye first. We never leave each other without saying goodbye."

He says, smiling.

They make their way to the living room and stand outside.

James knocks on the door.

"Love?"

He calls through.

"That's me leaving now and I just wanted to say goodbye. I can't wait to see your dress. Kate said it's..."

He stifles a laugh.

"Nice."

He says, rolling his eyes at Kate.

"But I bet it's even more than that, I bet it's gorgeous,

love."

Jenny doesn't reply.
"Jennifer?"
He calls her again.
"Did you go to the bathroom?"
He looks to Kate.
"You did leave her in here, yeah?"
Kate nods.
"Yeah."

She doesn't like how this is looking. She is worried, thinking that Jenny has left; deciding that, she doesn't want to marry James after all and it was all Kate's fault. She shouldn't have opened her mouth.

"She just had to sit down for a minute and get herself together."
She says, trying not to let worry project in her voice.

James ignores the hairs that prickle up on the back of his neck.
"Love, I'm gonna come in and spoil the surprise, if I don't get an answer."
He laughs.
"So, on three? 1, 2, 3... bye, love."

Still no response from Jenny and Kate starts to fidget beside James.
"Maybe she's saving her voice, for her vows."
She says, trying to find any reason – besides running away – that she isn't answering back.

James shakes his head.
"She wouldn't ignore me, Kate."
"Then... maybe–"
"I'm going in, Kate."
She grabs hold of his arm.
"Don't."

In Her Shadow

She says softly.

"It's bad luck."

She frees his arm, expecting him to do as she says but he turns the handle and steps inside.

Silence falls around them like a ton of bricks as they focus their eyes on Jenny.

She is sitting in the armchair, eyes closed and a half smile on her face. Almost — James thinks — like a painting of herself and not the real thing. His own 'Mona Lisa'.

"Jennifer... Jennifer..."

He says, taking tiny steps towards her.

He knows she isn't sleeping and Kate catches onto that too but James isn't ready to face — or to believe in — the reality just yet.

"Well, I've seen the dress now, haven't I?"

He says, with a nervous laugh.

"I've gone and spoiled it."

Kate places her hands on his shoulders.

"Don't do this to yourself, James."

He shrugs her off.

"What are you talking about, Kate? She's just — she's just... you're having a little nap, aren't you, love?"

He says to Jenny.

"Don't blame you. It's a big - it's our wedding day."

He runs his hands through his hair.

"James..."

Kate whimpers.

"Shut up, Kate! Just close your mouth!"

He snaps.

"You don't get to do this."

He doesn't know what to do..

"It's too soon."

He whispers, and he falls to his knees and stares at Jenny.

"It's a very puffy dress, love."

He says, as he loosens his tie and tries to stave off a panic attack.

"You – you – you haven't... you can't. Jennifer, you can't."

He starts to hyperventilate and Kate kneels down behind him and wraps her arms around his trembling body.

"1, 2, 3, 4, 5."

She whispers.

"Count. 1, 2, 3, 4, 5."

James starts to count along with her to calm himself down and in the midst of the commotion, they don't hear the front door opening.

"Tell you what, it's cold out there. Isn't it, Dahlia?"

James throws himself across the room and slams the door in Dahlia and Richard's face.

"What's all this about?"

Richard tries to push his way in and Kate leans against the door with James.

"She can't come in."

She says, her voices shaking.

"Take her away, Richard."

Richard stops pushing and there's silence on the other side. Not even Dahlia speaks.

"Richard..."

James sobs.

"Richard, mate... that's it."

He sinks all the way to the floor and releases all of his tears. Kate sits beside him and squeezes his arm.

"We have to-"

"Not yet."

He says, cutting her off.

"They can't take her yet."

She is about to protest but is interrupted by the door,

creaking open.

"Kate."

Says Richard.

"Can you please go and sit with Dahlia in the room, while I talk to James."

She looks at James and he sits up.

"Could you, please?"

He asks her, wanting her to leave him with Richard.

She nods and squeezes past Richard and he takes a seat beside James and sighs.

"How are we going to do this?"

He asks him, not looking at his daughter.

"No, Richard... please."

James pleads.

"Not yet. Please, let me say goodbye."

He sniffs.

"She didn't even say goodbye."

He places a strong hand behind James' neck and squeezes.

"Son..."

He sighs.

"Not yet. Please, Richard?"

Richard nods.

"I'll be right outside."

He gets to his feet and leaves James alone in the room with Jenny. He didn't want to look at her himself and he couldn't find it in him to say goodbye to his only daughter but, he understood James' need to.

James sits himself at the side of the armchair – so he doesn't have to look at Jenny directly – and swallows back his tears.

"I don't think anyone likes 'goodbye'."

He starts.

"But nothing stings a person more than this type of... well, there's nothing good about it, love."

He says, not wanting to use the word 'goodbye' again.

"I – I looked through the rest of the scrapbook. I didn't understand the last page though... I was going to ask-"

He steals a quick glance at her and loses his train of thought.

"It's not fair."

He whispers.

"I shouldn't have to do this again."

He bangs the palm of his hand off of his forehead.

"That's so selfish, isn't it?"

He asks her.

"What about your dad? What about Da-"

His face crumples as he thinks about what Dahlia must be going through in the bedroom. Did she even understand?

"She will look after you..."

He says, sniffing and swallowing down a lump; which feels like tiny shards of glass.

"My mum. Wherever she is, she will look after you, okay?"

He reaches into his trouser pocket and pulls out a ring and squeezes it between his fingers.

"This was supposed to go to Kate..."

He sniffs.

"She's the oldest but-"

He kneels up close to her.

"It went to me instead."

He hesitates as he moves his hands towards her left hand but he wants her to have it so, he gathers all the strength he has left and slides it onto her ring finger.

He wants to hold onto her hand but it's far too cold. Too dead, he thinks and can't bring himself to do it.

"Forgive me, love."

He sighs.

"It's not you. It can't be you..."

Richard steps back into the room, still not letting his eyes land on Jenny.

"Son, we have to call them now."

James nods as he blinks away the saltiest tears he's ever cried.

"I know."

He says, shakily.

"I know."

Richard helps him up and leads him out of the living room.

"Dahlia is in the bedroom, if you want to go speak to her?"

Kate says, squeezing his shoulder.

"She's watching cartoons."

James wipes his face and takes a deep breath.

"What does she think is happening?"

He asks, not sure how he is going to tell her.

"She thinks you and Jenny have had a falling out."

She replies.

He takes another deep breath and steps into the bedroom.

Dahlia sits in a little, blue dress and has her hair all braided. She looks so sweet and it just breaks James' heart.

"That's a lovely dress, love."

He says, sinking beside her.

"Your hair is very pretty too."

She smiles.

"Daddy said mommy could never do braids so he always did it."

She says.

"Is mommy's hair braided?"

He sniffs back some tears.

"Love..."

"Why are you sad?"

She wonders.

"Is mommy's dress too small?"
He shakes his head and bites his lip.
"Thing is..."
He takes a deep breath.
"Your mummy-"
"She doesn't want to be the queen?"
Dahlia innocently asks.
"Yes, love."
He steadies his voice.
"She wanted more than anything to be the queen today but..."
She pats his head.
"The stars need her?"
She asks, almost as if she knows.
James' bottom lip trembles but he can't help feel warmed by her innocence.
"They do, love and it's not fair but, she had to leave before she – she... she had to leave."
Before she could say anything else, James scoops her up into his arms and holds onto her tight. She doesn't hug him back; not understanding what's really going on and he's glad she doesn't but, he didn't want to be the one to do this.
"She can't come back, love."
He whispers.
"She's gone."
She wraps her little arms around his neck and squeezes now.
They cry together and let whatever is going on – outside of the bedroom – go on without them.
Dahlia cries herself into a sleep and as James tucks her in; he kisses her forehead and can swear that, he feels Jenny there beside him but when he turns to smile at her, no one is there.
He hangs his head, knowing this is something he will never

get used to. He will always look for her – expecting her to be there – and when he's met with an empty space beside him, it will never get any easier.

There's a faint knocking on the bedroom door and when James opens it, he is aghast to find William on the other side.

"Not today, Will."

He huffs.

"You–"

"I'm here to offer my condolences and take Dahlia home."

He says, hovering in the doorway.

"I mean no harm, James."

James lets him inside.

"Don't wake her."

He says, softly.

"She's so peaceful."

William nods.

"Does she know?"

He asks.

"Not exactly."

James replies.

"She knows that Jennifer can't come back but–"

He tries to hold back his tears, not wanting William to see him cry.

"She doesn't know why."

William's eyes start to fill too.

"I'm a terrible person."

He sighs.

"I made her life–"

"Not the time to throw yourself a pity party, Will." Says James, wiping his face.

"I read that book, anyway. I know what you did, I know how the story ends."

William shakes his head.

In Her Shadow

"She's got her lips."

He says.

James thinks he is talking about Dahlia and he nods.

"Her eyes too."

He points out.

"No."

William says, taking a deep breath.

"I mean June. No one kissed me like Jenny and when she left me-"

"Don't."

James whispers.

"Don't you dare. You don't get to try and justify-"
"That's not what I'm doing."

Argues William.

"I'm just trying to – to – I know what you're going through."

He says, finally.

"There'll never be anyone like her – like Jenny – and -"

"Difference is-"

James cuts in.

"I won't be searching for someone like her – or anyone for that matter –."

William nods.

"Of course."

He says, feeling hopeless.

"I'm not trying to-"

"Then don't."

Says James, shaking his head.

"Just leave."

He gestures to the door.

"You're not welcome here."

William swallows the lump that has formed in his throat and nods.

"I'm sorry."

He whispers, before exiting the room.

"I'm sorry."

James gently closes the door behind him and curls up beside Dahlia. He tries not to cry but the tears won't stop falling and before he too falls into a sleep, he takes one last look at the little girl and smiles.

As long as he gets to still see her; Jenny won't be gone completely, he thinks. There's still a huge part of her left here and he won't let go of it easy.

He is 'daddy two'.

Chapter 22: A Girl Called 'Love'

It's the day of Jenny's funeral and James takes his place in front of the podium and looks out to the loved ones, who have showed up to say goodbye to her.

He tries to give them a warming smile but his heart hurts too much so he just stares at them in bewilderment.

He clears his throat.

"Thank you all for coming today."

He says, finally.

"It means so-"

He takes a deep breath and tries to stop more tears from staining his face. He needs to do this; he's been practicing this for a few days now and he doesn't want to let Jenny down.

He fixes his gaze on the wall at the back. Deciding it's best if he doesn't make direct eye contact with anyone – especially Dahlia – who doesn't quite understand the concept of death and doesn't realise that her mother is in that wooden box, that sits just in front of her.

James would love to see the whole thing through her eyes, to have her innocence and to not know that this was final. Jenny isn't living on in the stars, having tea party's with his mother. She is lying – in the coffin before him – and soon, she will be lying in the ground.

He straightens his back and continues.

"I have everything that I want to say written down on these little pieces of paper here."

He holds them up, with a trembling hand.

"But now that it's time to say them... I'm afraid."

He steals a quick glance at Dahlia.

"Not all of us who are here today understand what this day means, what it symbolizes and that's not necessarily a bad thing – given what this day is marking – but I don't want to be the one who points it out. Forgive me. I just can't do that."

He manages to show Dahlia a smile, he couldn't quite muster before and decides that he won't speak of Jenny like she is gone and instead, will speak of her as if she were in the room; smiling at him and encouraging him to carry on.

He applies this method – not only for Dahlia's sake – but for the sake of his sanity also. He knows the crowd will understand.

"Jenny – to me – is my yellow brick road."

He starts.

"I will follow her anywhere and she always helps me overcome any obstacles on the way. She always keeps the path smooth and bump free; journeying with her is always pleasant."

He coughs, trying to stop his voice from breaking.

"She is the fire that keeps me warm in winter and she mesmerises me, with her pretty flames of love and adoration. She never lets me go cold."

He sneaks another peek at Dahlia, who watches him – attentively – as if he were reading her her favourite fairy tale.

"She is mother to the most beautiful, little girl and-" He starts to choke at this part.

"And-"

William, who has been holding back his tears, let's them fall freely now. One after another, after another.

"You're doing good, James. Keep going."

He says, encouragingly.

James nods and sniffs back tears of his own. He knew William had to be there today for Dahlia but he would rather, he didn't have to communicate with him.

In Her Shadow

"Jenny always said to me; 'baby, that girl has magic in her eyes', when speaking of Dahlia."

He powers on.

"She said she saw the world as it was supposed to be. Fantastical, bright... innocent. And I'd say 'so do you, love. Your eyes are magic too'."

He breathes out, trying to keep his voice steady and clear.

"She seen me as I am supposed to be – as no one else could see me – and she made me feel worthy.

She gave me a home, when I didn't have one."

He shakes his head.

"I don't mean floors, walls and a roof. I mean in her heart, she built a home there for me."

He chews on the inside of his cheeks.

"I will not say goodbye."

He says, wringing his hands.

"I will not search for another home, where I can lay my hat."

He takes a deep breath.

"I will cling to her memory – like a barnacle clings to a boat – and wait for her to call me back, to that very same home she assembled for me – for us – there."

He touches his heart and smiles.

"When the sun is shining, I'll know she is smiling and I will smile too; as I sit contently in the shade."

He fidgets with the pieces of paper in front of him.

"I would like to end with a poem I wrote for Jennifer, if that's okay?"

He looks to Richard, who nods in encouragement.

He continues.

"I know a girl, I call her 'love'
not because I have forgotten her name,
but because she is the epitome of the word

and to this lonesome candle, she brought a flame.
Her eyes are green like the kind of trees
that still thrive in the wintertime,
and I wish I let her know
before the stars needed her to shine;
I think you are a Goddess."

He repeats the last line, directly to the coffin.

"I think you are a Goddess."

The room fills with the sound of soft sniffing, as the crowd try not to break down and James is about to take a seat, when a new sound catches him by surprise. The sound of a small pair of hands, clapping together in applause.

Dahlia stands, clapping louder and louder and grins from ear to ear.

"Mommy the Goddess of the stars!"

She shouts.

He walks to her and whisks her up into his arms. Although he feels weak, Dahlia feels light as a feather to him and he never wants to put her down.

William pats him on the back.

"That was very inspiring."

He says.

"I take my hat off to you."

James doesn't even look at him. He doesn't care what he thinks as the only thing – the only people – who matter to him are Dahlia and Richard. Dahlia hangs onto him and Richard squeezes his arm and smiles. Their approval – their acceptance of him – is all that matters.

When the service is over, they drive to Jenny's final resting place and form a half circle around her coffin.

James thought he would never be able to help carry it but he stood tall and gave it all of the strength he had. The coffin – if it were something of a magicians box, with an assistant inside – would not be the least bit heavy. The fact that it held James' world inside though, was a different matter.

It was like carrying a box made of steel and the person inside was made of lead.

"Ashes to ashes and dust to dust."

James doesn't hear the rest and when it comes his time to throw dirt on the coffin, his instinct is to throw himself on there with it.

"I'm not your ball and chain."

He hears, repeatedly in his mind and he manages to back away and let them lower her down. 'Return her to the earth'.

Dahlia watches in wonder. She still isn't aware that her mother is in the box and she's too shy to ask anyone what's in there so, she saves this question for later. She will ask her father and it seems, not even he will be able to give her the real answer. He stands to the side, on his own as Dahlia has made her way over to James and is holding his hand. Richard stands behind them and the rest of the crowd seem to be on his side too.

James throws a glance at William and for the first time, he pities him. He didn't want to but today is a hard enough day, without recounting or rehashing any of the other stuff. He nods and throws him a smile and William nods back. He knows James will never forgive him and they will never be best friends but they both owed it to Jenny to be civil, for Dahlia's sake.

She loves them both and thinks them both her father so, neither of them will make trouble for each other; from this point on. They will focus all that energy into giving Dahlia the best upbringing they can. One that Jenny would be proud of.

On the drive home, James can't really get his head straight. He was going to go to Richard's home, with Dahlia for a little while but he just needed to spend some time on his own.

In Her Shadow

As he pulls up outside of the place he shared with Jenny, he's not sure about going inside. He's not ready to be faced with silence and empty spaces – which Jenny would normally fill – yet.

He rests his head on the steering wheel and cries – what feels like one million – salty tears and as each one falls, he doesn't rush to wipe them away. He lets them stain his face – he almost wants them to – and lets every lump that rises in his throat, manifest in a heart wrenching sob.

His heart is broken.

Not figuratively. His heart is literally in pieces and nothing anyone could say or do, will help fit those pieces back together again.

He takes a deep breath and as he exhales, he steps outside of the car and prepares himself to go inside.

Every light is still on as he didn't want to come back to darkness and the first scent to hit him, is Jenny's perfume; a concoction of vanilla and daisy chains. He doesn't know if he is smelling it now because he wanted to or that, it really did linger on as if it had just been sprayed. Either way, he takes a moment to just lean back and breath it in.

It soothes him – albeit for five minutes or so – and he shuffles on and into the living room.

He eases himself onto the sofa and lets his gaze wander across to the armchair. He wants – in this instant – to get up and throw it across the room. As if it were the cause of Jenny's demise as this was the last thing to hold her.

He lets that thought go.

Instead – he decides – he will keep the chair, for that very reason. It was the last thing that held her – supported her – and made sure that she left this world peacefully. Comfortably.

His eyes flicker to the side of the armchair. He thinks about the things he said while he sat with Jenny and wonders

In Her Shadow

if some part of her had hung back, just to hear them. He hoped she wasn't gone completely in that moment, that she felt his hand take her hand for the last time and that she was happy with the ring. The wedding ring.

She still got to wear it and she still got to wear the dress as he sat beside her in white. The show still went on...

he starts to unbutton his shirt – not wanting to stay in those funeral clothes any longer – and when he looks for a new shirt to pull on; the first one his hands find, belongs to Jenny. The same shirt that he had worn on the day; she said she would marry him.

He bites his lip and without thinking twice, he pulls it over his head and stretches it onto his body; keeping her essence with him, a little while longer.

He can't imagine how he is going to cope without her as, all he can think about right now is; curling up into a little ball and letting the world move on without him. He didn't want to be a part of it anymore – he didn't want to fall asleep and dream – if Jenny wasn't beside him.

He drags his feet all the way to the kitchen. He doesn't know why as, he doesn't feel like he could eat or drink anything but he knew he wasn't prepared to go to the bedroom yet. Their bedroom.

He takes a seat at the breakfast table and looks across to the empty chair in front of him. That chair – he thinks – he can definitely throw that chair across the room but, he won't. He remains seated and lets out a heavy sigh.

"Shall I make us a coffee, love?"

He whispers.

"It's cold out there."

He knew he wasn't going to get a reply but he doesn't think he will ever stop asking this or ever stop acting, like she is there.

In Her Shadow

How do you just let a person go completely? He wonders.

He certainly didn't do it with his mother. Part of him still liked to believe that she wasn't really gone either that; she was back in London and hadn't figured out how to use the latest technology and so, he didn't hear from her.

He didn't care how absurd that was. He would do the same with Jenny, he decides. Maybe he could picture her somewhere else, somewhere where there was lots of sun and her skin would be tanned and not as pale and ghost like as it was.

"Ghost like..."

His eyes start to tear up again as he finds it difficult to paint this scene in his mind. All he can see is Jenny, sitting in the arm chair and not moving – not breathing – and her skin as cold as ice.

He couldn't apply the same method here. Jenny is really gone and as hard of a pill that is to swallow, he must do it anyway.

He pulls the shirt up to his face and breathes it in, before he ruins it with his scent.

Sleep seems to find him shortly after and as he dreams; the world keeps spinning, even if he doesn't want to accept it's so.

The show must go on.

In Her Shadow

Epilogue

It's a wet and windy day in December – four days before Christmas – and James finds himself; walking through the park that he, Jenny and Dahlia had their picnic in.

He looks for the bench where they all sat – the one that reminded him of the bench he sat on with his mother – and he takes a seat. He doesn't care that it is wet, he doesn't care if he catches a nasty cold or hypothermia. He just wants to sit there and remember.

He looks out to the water and wonders where all of the ducks have gone. Not a single one is to be found and although that's not what he is here for – to feed the ducks – it disappoints him a little.

He sighs.

"Probably flew somewhere warm."

He says, tucking his hands into his pockets.

He forgets that just days before, he ripped out the last page of Jenny's scrapbook and kept it in his right pocket; to look at, whenever he got the chance.

He still didn't understand what it meant.

It held a picture of him in the middle and around it; Jenny had coloured every inch of the page, in black crayon. To anyone who didn't know her, they would think it was quite a troubling imagine but there was something about it, that made James smile.

He never really liked how he looked and Jenny was forever taking photos of him and he used to cover his face or take the camera from her and delete them but not with this image. He looked happy in this picture – almost like he posed for it –

and he couldn't think why.

He traces his fingers across it and a little movie starts to play out in his mind.

First he sees Jenny; laughing and pulling funny faces and then it cuts to him, sitting on the ground and looking up at her.

"For me, please?"

He hears her say.

"Okay, but just one."

He remembers now. She asked that he smile for the camera and after protesting for a long two minutes, he finally gave in.

although it was for Jenny, his smile wasn't forced. He remembers her smiling down at him — a contagious smile — and he couldn't help but to smile back.

That explains the happy picture, he thinks. But what about the rest of the page? Why all the black?

He sighs again and tucks it back into his pocket.

The water starts to ripple as rain falls heavily and splishes and splashes into it. He doesn't move. The rain never really bothered him anyway.

He turns his head up to the sky and closes his eyes and the rain falls upon his face, like tiny daggers made of ice.

He enjoys the sting.

It's a reminder that he can still feel as; for awhile there, he started to shut down. Like a robot needing to be repaired, he couldn't function - he couldn't feel a thing.

Not even the little, warm hands that Dahlia pressed against his cheeks when she was giving him Eskimo kisses.

He hated that.

He wanted desperately for her every little hug, every little giggle and every little smile; to reach right into the heart of him and squeeze it. She didn't deserve to be met with the shell that he hid away in.

In Her Shadow

He drops his head and shakes the rain from his hair and is about to leave when a strange image paints itself, on the walls of his mind.

He sees his mother sitting on the bench they used to go to but this time, when he takes his seat beside her; he is a grown man. This isn't a memory, this was a wish that his heart constantly made and suddenly, he feels tears rolling down his face.

He didn't understand why he had to lose the two women he loved the most – the two people he loved the most – there was no one like them on this earth and now he was all alone.

Richard has been treating him like he is part of the family and Dahlia still calls him 'daddy two' but he still felt that loneliness. A loneliness that only a mother or the love from a soulmate could cure.

He stretches his hand across to the other side of the bench and chokes up further, when he finds it empty.

He was still in that place where, he thought that maybe he would wake up any minute and none of it would be real. His mother would still be dancing in the kitchen and Jenny would be sitting beside him.

He moves his hand further across and drags it back slowly and as he does this, he feels a roughness, where there should be smoothness.

He looks down and is surprised to see that someone has carved something into the bench. He rolls his eyes, upset that someone could taint the happy memories on this bench with graffiti and he doesn't want to read it but, curiosity gets the better of him.

He shifts to get a better view and he bites his lip as he reads.

"You are the light, baby! - J"

He half laughs and half cries as he realises, this is a

message from Jenny. He doesn't know when she would've found the time to carve it but he's glad that she did. He needed this and the fact that she knew he would return to this bench, overwhelmed him.

"My little vandal."

He whispers.

He takes the scrapbook page out once more and it becomes clear to him now. She wanted him to know that; he is the light – he always was the light – and that's the only thing she focused on, when everything else was dark.

His tears start to sting less as they sink into his cheeks. They were happy tears, tears that he couldn't cry before and now that he could; he knew that, things were going to be okay. He could get through this because one day, he will see Jenny again and when he does; he will take his place – just as he did before – in her shadow.

He smiles at the thought and his heart – broken in pieces on the day Jenny died – starts to vibrate and pull itself back together. Only Jenny could be the one to do that – to make his heart whole again – and before he leaves to return home; he raises two fingertips to his lips, kisses them and drops them onto Jenny's message. Her last words to him.

He can't help but keep wearing his smile on the drive home and as the rain slides down the windscreen, he can almost make the little tiny drops; form the image of Jenny's face - if he screws his eyes up and concentrates really hard -.

Everything – he thinks – is going to be just fine.

And it will be.

Contact

To get in touch with Marianne or to find out what she is going to write next; you can find her on Twitter or Instagram.
Twitter: @ZamBlackheart
Instagram: @RebelYell90

Printed in Great Britain
by Amazon.co.uk, Ltd.,
Marston Gate.